PENGUIN TWENTIETH-CENTURY CLASSICS

THE STREET OF CROCODILES

Bruno Schulz was one of the most remarkably gifted writers to have been produced in Eastern Europe in this century. Little known outside his native Poland, his work nevertheless—and despite official disapproval—continues to exercise a profound influence over young Polish writers. His life and work are discussed in the Translator's Preface and in Jerzy Ficowski's Introduction, written especially for this Penguin edition. Penguin Books also publishes Bruno Schulz's *Sanatorium under the Sign of the Hourglass.*

Jerzy Ficowski is a poet, translator, and essayist. Born in 1924, he studied philosophy at the University of Warsaw. An early admirer of Bruno Schulz's prose, Ficowski was dedicated to finding Schulz's letters, which was a difficult task, since the majority of the addressees did not survive the war. In 1956 Ficowski published a book about Schulz, *The Regions of Great Heresy,* and in 1975 he edited the collection of Schulz's letters. Jerzy Ficowski lives in Warsaw.

To access Great Books Foundation Discussion Guides online, visit our Web site at www.penguin.com or the foundation Web site at www.greatbooks.org.

The Street of Crocodiles

BRUNO SCHULZ
Translated by Celina Wieniewska

Introduction by Jerzy Ficowski
Introduction translated by Michael Kandel

PENGUIN BOOKS

Published by the Penguin Group

Penguin Group (USA) Inc., 375 Hudson Street, New York, New York 10014, U.S.A.

Penguin Group (Canada), 90 Eglinton Avenue East, Suite 700, Toronto,
    Ontario, Canada M4P 2Y3 (a division of Pearson Penguin Canada Inc.)

Penguin Books Ltd, 80 Strand, London WC2R 0RL, England

Penguin Ireland, 25 St Stephen's Green, Dublin 2, Ireland (a division of Penguin Books Ltd)

Penguin Group (Australia), 250 Camberwell Road, Camberwell,
    Victoria 3124, Australia (a division of Pearson Australia Group Pty Ltd)

Penguin Books India Pvt Ltd, 11 Community Centre, Panchsheel Park, New Delhi – 110 017, India

Penguin Group (NZ), cnr Airborne and Rosedale Roads,
    Albany, Auckland 1310, New Zealand (a division of Pearson New Zealand Ltd)

Penguin Books (South Africa) (Pty) Ltd, 24 Sturdee Avenue,
    Rosebank, Johannesburg 2196, South Africa

Penguin Books Ltd, Registered Offices: 80 Strand, London WC2R 0RL, England

Originally published in Poland with the title
Cinnamon Shops 1934
English translation first published in the
United States of America by Walker and Company 1963
Published in Penguin Books 1977

30 29 28 27 26 25

Originally published in Penguin Books as part of the
"Writers from the Other Europe" series (general editor: Philip Roth)

LIBRARY OF CONGRESS CATALOGING IN PUBLICATION DATA
Schulz, Bruno, 1892–1942.
The street of crocodiles.
Translation of Sklepy cynamonowe.
I. Title. II. Series
{PZ3.S39St7} {PG7158.s2941}   891.8'5'37   76-48335
ISBN 0 14 01.8625 5

Printed in the United States of America
Set in Videocomp Garamond

The characters in these stories are fictitious, and any resemblance to actual
persons, living or dead, is purely coincidental.

Contents

Contents

Translator's Preface

He was small, unattractive and sickly, with a thin angular body and brown, deep-set eyes in a pale triangular face. He taught art at a secondary school for boys at Drogobych in southeastern Poland, where he spent most of his life. He had few friends outside his native city. In his leisure hours—of which there were probably many— he made drawings and wrote endlessly, nobody quite knew what. At the age of forty, having received an introduction through friends to Zofia Nałkowska, a distinguished novelist in Warsaw, he sent her some of his stories. They were published in 1934 under the title of *Cinnamon Shops*—and the name of Bruno Schulz was made. Three years later, a further collection of stories, with drawings by the author, *Sanatorium under the Sign of the Hourglass,* was published; then *The Comet,* a novella, appeared in a leading literary weekly. In between, Schulz made a translation of Kafka's *The Trial.* It is said that he was working on a novel entitled *The Messiah,* but nothing has remained of it. This is the sum total of his literary output.

After his literary success, he continued to live at Drogobych. The outbreak of World War II found him there. Together with other Jews of the city, he was confined to the ghetto and, according to some reports, "protected" by a Gestapo officer who liked his drawings.

One day in 1942, he ventured with a special pass to the "Aryan" quarter, was recognized by another SS man, a rival of his protector, and was shot dead in the street.

When Bruno Schulz's stories were reissued in Poland in 1957, translated into French and German, and acclaimed everywhere by a new generation of readers to whom he was unknown, attempts were made to place his œuvre in the mainstream of Polish literature, to find affinities, derivations, to explain him in terms of one literary theory or another. The task is well nigh impossible. He was a solitary man, living apart, filled with his dreams, with memories of his childhood, with an intense, formidable inner life, a painter's imagination, a sensuality and responsiveness to physical stimuli which most probably could find satisfaction only in artistic creation— a volcano, smoldering silently in the isolation of a sleepy provincial town.

The world of Schulz is basically a private world. At its center is his father—"that incorrigible improviser . . . the lonely hero who alone had waged war against the fathomless, elemental boredom that strangled the city." Father, bearded, sometimes resembling a biblical prophet, is one of the great eccentrics of literature. In reality he was a Drogobych merchant, who had inherited a textile business and ran it until illness forced him to abandon it to the care of his wife. He then retired to ten years of enforced idleness and his own world of dreams. Father surrounds himself with ledgers and pores over them for days on end—while in reality all he is doing is putting colored decals on the ruled pages; Father who has zoological interest, who imports eggs of rare species of birds and has them hatched in his attic, who is dominated by the blue-eyed servant girl, Adela; who believes that tailors' dummies should be treated with as much respect as human beings; Father who loathes cockroaches to the point of fascination; who in a last apotheosis rises above the vulgar mob of buyers and sellers and, drowning in rivers of cloth, blows the horn of Atonement. . . . Then there is Mother, who did not love her husband properly and who condemned him therefore to an existence on the periphery of life, because he was not rooted in any woman's heart. There are uncles and aunts and cousins, each described with deadly accuracy, with epithets as from a clinical diagnosis.

These were Schulz's people, the people of Drogobych, at one time the Klondike of Galicia when oil was struck near the city and prosperity entered it and destroyed the old patriarchal way of life, bringing false values, bogus Americanization, and new ways of making a quick fortune—when the white spaces of an old map of the city were transformed into a new district, when the Street of Crocodiles became its center, peopled with a race of rattleheaded men and women of easy morals. The old dignity of the cinnamon shops, with their aroma of spices and distant countries, changed into something brash, second-rate, questionable, slightly suspect.

One could continue to quote from the stories: somebody might perhaps attempt a psychoanalysis of Schulz on the basis of his writings. Polish and other critics have drawn attention to the influence that Thomas Mann, Freud, and Kafka exercised on him. This may or may not be true: although it is also said that Schulz first read *The Trial* when the book was sent to him for reviewing *after* the publication of *Cinnamon Shops*. What is undoubtedly true is that the atmosphere of both Kafka's and Schulz's lives in their respective provinces is not dissimilar. These distant outposts of the former Austro-Hungarian empire, with the memories of the "good" Emperor Francis Joseph still a living tradition, looked up to Vienna as the center of cultural and artistic life much more than to Prague or Warsaw.

But whether or not these derivations existed in fact does not really matter, the stories still speak for themselves in the same voice as in the 1930s and there emerges from them in a sunken world, lost forever under the lava of history, an ordinary provincial city with ordinary people going about their daily tasks, a city scorched by the hot summers of every school child's holidays, sometimes shaken by unexpected high winds from the mountains, but mostly sleepy and lethargic—here brought to life by the magic touch of a poetic genius, in a prose as memorable, powerful and unique as are the brushstrokes of Marc Chagall.

Introduction

On November 19, 1942, on the streets of Drogobych, a small provincial town that belonged to Poland
before World War II (and now is in the U.S.S.R.), there
commenced a so-called action carried out by the local
sections of the SS and the Gestapo against the Jewish
population. This was a relatively minor incident in an
enormous genocidal undertaking; the day of November
19, remembered by a few surviving inhabitants of
Drogobych as "Black Thursday," brought death to some
one hundred and fifty passersby. Among the murdered
who lay until nightfall on the sidewalks of the little town
—who lay where the bullets reached them—was Bruno
Schulz, a former teacher of drawing at the local high
school. In vain had Polish writers, together with under-
ground organizations, attempted to come to his rescue
while he was still alive. They had furnished him with false
papers and money to enable him to escape and hide in
a safe place, but an attempt to escape was never made. At
night, under cover of dark, a friend of the dead man
carried his body to the nearby Jewish cemetery and buried him.

No trace remains of that cemetery, and the manu-
scripts of Schulz's unpublished works, given to someone
for safekeeping, are lost. They disappeared along with
their custodian. Thus perished, with a portion of his liter-

ary œuvre, one of the finest Polish writers of our century.

Bruno Schulz was the author of two books published before the war—*Cinnamon Shops* (1934), which has been translated into English and published under the title *The Street of Crocodiles,* and *Sanatorium under the Sign of the Hourglass* (1937)—works that were recognized immediately by the Polish literary critics and honored by the Polish Academy of Literature, although they were discovered by the world only many years later. The literature of reborn Poland in the twenty-year period between the two great wars abounded in outstanding authors such as Stanisław Ignacy Witkiewicz and Witold Gombrowicz, who are today widely known and translated into many languages, but first and foremost is Schulz, who is a phenomenon thoroughly apart in the sphere of Polish literature. In its outline the biography of Bruno Schulz appears unassuming and bare. This bard of his native town never left the streets of Drogobych for long. For almost twenty years he worked there as a teacher of drawing and handicrafts, otherwise leading the life of a recluse and maintaining contact with those near to him through letters. In this way he alleviated his isolation without having it disturbed by any outside presence. These letters to his friends, so few of whom survived the war, were in fact the genesis of his writing; for a period they constituted his sole literary activity. In other respects the topography of his life's journey is uneventful. His art grew out of his perceptions of his native town and his childhood.

He was born July 12, 1892, into a merchant family. His father, Jakub, was a bookkeeper and owner of a dry-goods shop, a shop that later was to become in the son's writing the repository of an elaborate fantasy, the sanctum of Schulzian mythology. This mythic resurrection of the shop and the reconstruction of childhood with all its emotional riches would take place only after the father and the business were long gone.

Schulz's Drogobych was a town in Galicia, a province of the Austro-Hungarian empire, which more than a hundred years earlier had helped to eradicate Poland from the map of Europe. In this part of the conquered land Bruno Schulz—the youngest of three children, educated at home and in a school named after Emperor Francis Joseph—did not grow up in the dominant traditions of German-speaking Austria, nor did he remain in the sphere of traditional Jewish culture. The merchant profession to which his parents belonged separated them from the Hasidim, and he was never to learn the language of his ancestors. Bruno Schulz did know German fluently, but he wrote in Polish, the language nearest to him and most obedient to his pen.

When Poland regained independent statehood in 1918, Schulz was twenty-six years old and had had three years of study—discontinued just before the war—in architecture. He taught himself to draw and produced graphics, intending to gain proficiency in this field and make it his career. His work in fine arts gave evidence of considerable talent but enabled him only to obtain—and with difficulty, at that—the post of a drawing-master in a high school. His ideas for fiction date from the 1920s. They mark the beginning, with a delay of some years yet before his publishing debut, of the life of Schulz the writer, who was to find the duties of a teacher utterly repugnant, although that job furnished his sole means of support.

In the days crammed with lessons he devoted his free

moments to conversing with friends about art—not with the local friends he met daily and who never even suspected him of literary aspirations, but with those distant correspondents living in other cities who were confidants of his dialogues on art. These epistolary conversations provided him for years with his only real spiritual contact with other people. For a long time he did not let anyone know of his literary efforts; it was only drawing and painting that he practiced openly, in full view of his friends, despite the obviously masochistic theme of many of his works. His first literary compositions he concealed in a drawer, sharing them with no one.

Lacking the courage to address *readers,* he tried at first to write for *a* reader, a recipient of his letters. When at last, around 1930, he found a partner for this exchange in the person of Deborah Vogel, a poet and doctor of philosophy who lived in Lvov, his letters—even then often masterpieces of the epistolary art—underwent a metamorphosis, becoming daring fragments of dazzling prose. His correspondent, greatly excited, urged him to continue. It was in this way, letter by letter, piece by piece, that *The Street of Crocodiles* came into being, a literary work enclosed a few pages at a time in envelopes and dropped into the mailbox. Surely no other work of belles-lettres has originated in so curious and, at the same time, so natural a manner. A few more years had to pass before—thanks to the support of the eminent novelist Zofia Nałkowska—the resistance of publishers to a work so innovative could be overcome and *The Street of Crocodiles* could appear in book form. So the book was made available to the public, although it had been conceived and executed with only one reader in mind, the addressee of the letters sent from Drogobych to Lvov. Writing in this way, Schulz could be wholly indifferent to the tastes of the literary coterie and the capricious demands of the official critics. He would experience their pressures later on, and more than once he claimed that they paralyzed him, changing the quiet immediacy of personal communication into work fraught with peril and addressed to the Unknown—and this for one to whom art was a confession of faith, faith in the demiurgic role of myth.

What is this Schulzian mythopoeia, this mythologizing of reality? On what was his artistic purpose to "mature into childhood" based? Childhood here is understood as the stage when each sensation is accompanied by an inventive act of the imagination, when reality, not yet systematized by experience, "submits" to new associations, assumes the forms suggested to it, and comes to life fecund with dynamic visions; childhood is a stage when etiological myths are born at every step. It is precisely there, in the mythmaking realm, that both the source and the final goal of Bruno Schulz's work reside.

From sublime spheres the Schulzian myth sinks to the depths of ordinary existence; or, if you will, what Schulz gives us is the mythological Ascension of the Everyday. The myth takes on human shape, and simultaneously the reality made mythical becomes more nonhuman than ever before. Conjecture easily changes into certainty, the obvious into illusion; possibilities *materialize*. Myth stalks the streets of Drogobych, turning ragamuffins playing tiddledywinks into enchanted soothsayers who read the future in the cracks of a wall, or transforming a shopkeeper into a prophet or a goblin. Art was to Schulz "a short circuit of sense between words, a sudden regeneration of the primal myths." Schulz said: "All poetry is mythmaking; it strives to recreate the myths about the world."

Thomas Mann's *Joseph and His Brothers,* Schulz's favorite work, is an excellent example of the repeated patterns, the stories that return and return in different variations, continually reembodied from the earliest times up to the present day. Mann presents the biblical story "on a monumental scale"; Schulz, incorporating mythic archetypes within the confines of his own biography, unites his family to legend. His major work was to have been the lost novel titled *The Messiah,* in which the myth of the coming of the Messiah would symbolize a return to the happy perfection that existed at the beginning—in Schulzian terms, the return to childhood.

Schulzian time—his mythic time—obedient and submissive to man, offers artistic recompense for the profaned time of everyday life, which relentlessly subordinates all things to itself and carries events and people off in a current of evanescence. Schulz introduces a subjective, psychological time and then gives it substance, objectivity, by subjecting the course of occurrences to its laws. The reckoning of time by the calendar is likewise called into question. It can happen, writes Schulz, that "in a run of normal uneventful years that great eccentric, Time, begets sometimes other years, different, prodigal years which—like a sixth, smallest toe—grow a thirteenth freak month." Schulz's fantasies—dazzling, full of the paradoxical and the plausible—are "apocrypha, put secretly between the chapters of the great book of the year." They are Schulz's mythological supplement to the calendar, and when he wishes that the stories about his father, smuggled into the pages of his old calendar, would there grow equal in authority to its true text, he is expressing his own not merely artistic desire to materialize the yearnings of the imagination, to impart to its creations an objective reality, to erase the boundary between fact and dream.

"Should I tell you that my room is walled up? . . . In what way might I leave it?" asks Schulz. "Here is how: Goodwill knows no obstacle; nothing can stand before a deep desire. I have only to imagine a door, a door old and good, like in the kitchen of my childhood, with an iron latch and bolt. There is no room so walled up that it will not open with such a trusty door, if you have but the strength to insinuate it." On one side of that door lies life and its restricted freedom, on the other—art. That *door* leads from the captivity of Bruno, a timid teacher of arts and crafts, to the freedom of Joseph, the hero of *The Street of Crocodiles*.

This is the credo of Bruno Schulz—of the Great Heresiarch who imposed new measurements on time, in this way taking his revenge on life. Yet from behind the mythological faith of the writer there peers, again and again, the mocking grin of reality, revealing the ephemeral nature of the fictions that seek to contend with it.

Many of Schulz's theoretical statements express with precision and accuracy the ideas behind his work, its foundations, and its psychological and philosophical motivations. In response to the questions of the famous Polish writer, philosopher, painter, and playwright Witkiewicz, his friend, Schulz said: "I do not know just how in childhood we arrive at certain images, images of crucial significance to us. They are like filaments in a solution around which the sense of the world crystallizes for us. . . . They are meanings that seem predestined for us, ready and waiting at the very entrance of our life . . . . Such images constitute a program, establish our soul's fixed fund of capital, which is allotted to us very early in the form of inklings and half-conscious feelings. It seems to me that the rest of our life passes in the interpretation of those insights, in the attempt to master them with all the wisdom we acquire, to draw them through all the range of intellect we have in our possession. These early images mark the boundaries of an artist's creativity. His creativity is a deduction from assumptions already made. He cannot now discover anything new; he learns only to understand more and more the secret entrusted to him at the beginning, and his art is a constant exegesis, a commentary on that single verse that was assigned him. But art will never unravel that secret completely. The secret remains insoluble. The knot in which the soul was bound is no trick knot, coming apart with a tug at its end. On the contrary, it grows tighter and tighter. We work at it, untying, tracing the path of the string, seeking the end, and out of this manipulating comes art. . . .

"To what genre does *The Street of Crocodiles* belong? How should it be classified? I consider it an autobiographical novel, not merely because it is written in the first person and one can recognize in it certain events and experiences from the author's own childhood. It is an autobiography—or rather, a genealogy—of the spirit . . . since it reveals the spirit's pedigree back to those depths where it merges with mythology, where it becomes lost in mythological ravings. I have always felt that the roots of the individual mind, if followed far enough down, would lose themselves in some mythic lair. This is the final depth beyond which one can no longer go."

Schulz's work is an expression of rebellion against the kingdom "of the quotidian, that fixing and delimiting of all possibilities, the guarantee of secure borders, within which art is once and for all time . . . closed off." Though mostly divided up into a series of stories, his writing taken as a whole has the character of a unified, consistent system, similar to systems of belief. His artistry is a unique sacral practice in which myths are accompanied by worship, ritual, and verbal ceremony. Schulz digs down, delving for the taproots, the seeds of our conceptions and imaginings, for, in his words, "the spawning bed of history." He says: "Just beyond our words . . . roar the dark and incommensurable elements. . . . Thus is accomplished within us a complete regression, a retreat to the interior, the return journey to the roots." The meddling with language, with semantics, in these depths, in order to give form to the inexpressible—that is the goal of Schulz's poetic search for definitions. Reading Rainer Maria Rilke, Schulz's most beloved poet, was for him a constant comfort, a source of moral support in his creative struggles. "The existence of his book," he wrote in a letter, "is a pledge that the tangled, mute masses of things unformulated within us may yet emerge to the surface miraculously distilled."

When Schulz's popularity as a writer threatened his privacy and solitude, his creative work began to slacken, and more and more frequently he fell into barren and agonizing states of depression. He spoke and wrote to his friends many times of the blessings of seclusion, seeing it as absolutely essential for his art, although at the same time he was painfully aware of his isolation. In reply to a letter, he wrote to one of his acquaintances: "You overrate the benefits of my Drogobych existence. What I lack here too, even here, is silence, my own musical silence, the tranquil pendulum subject only to its own gravitation, having a clear line of movement, not troubled by any foreign influence. This substantial silence—positive, full—is itself almost art. Those matters that wish, so I believe, to express themselves through me operate above a certain point of silence; they take form in an environment brought to perfect equilibrium." Elsewhere, speaking of *The Street of Crocodiles,* he confesses: "In a way these 'stories' are true; they represent my style of living, my particular lot. The dominant feature of that lot is a profound solitude, a withdrawal from the cares of daily life. Solitude is the catalyst that brings reality to fermentation, to the precipitating out of figures and colors."

Schulz's solitude was complex and many-sided, not merely the mode of life of an introvert who eschewed the clamor of the world. Both the small provincial town detached from the main currents of life and the writer's strange sense of identification with the Jewish community *condemned* him to some degree to isolation. That isolation was all the greater when, in view of his striking singularity, which the inhabitants of Drogobych saw as pathological deviation, he was cut off even from his fellow townspeople. His Jewishness too was problematic. In the eyes of those about him it was evident and undeniable, and yet he did not at all feel himself to be a full-fledged citizen of the ghetto. His ties with his own genealogy, marginal in the present, mainly had to do with prehistory, with the mythic ancestors in the mythic Bible of his own devising.

JERZY FICOWSKI

The Street of Crocodiles

August

1

In July my father went to take the waters and left me, with my mother and elder brother, a prey to the blinding white heat of the summer days. Dizzy with light, we dipped into that enormous book of holidays, its pages blazing with sunshine and scented with the sweet melting pulp of golden pears.

On those luminous mornings Adela returned from the market, like Pomona emerging from the flames of day, spilling from her basket the colorful beauty of the sun—the shiny pink cherries full of juice under their transparent skins, the mysterious black morellos that smelled so much better than they tasted; apricots in whose golden pulp lay the core of long afternoons. And next to that pure poetry of fruit, she unloaded sides of meat with their keyboard of ribs swollen with energy and strength, and seaweeds of vegetables like dead octopuses and squids—the raw material of meals with a yet undefined taste, the vegetative and terrestrial ingredients of dinner, exuding a wild and rustic smell.

The dark second-floor apartment of the house in Market Square was shot through each day by the naked heat of summer: the silence of the shimmering streaks of air, the squares of brightness dreaming their intense dreams on the floor; the sound of a barrel organ rising from the deepest golden vein of day; two or three bars of a chorus, played on a distant piano over and over again, melting in the sun on the white pavement, lost in the fire of high noon.

After tidying up, Adela would plunge the rooms into semidarkness by drawing down the linen blinds. All colors immediately fell an octave lower, the room filled with shadows, as if it had sunk to the bottom of the sea and the light was reflected in mirrors of green water—and the heat of the day began to breathe on the blinds as they stirred slightly in their daydreams.

On Saturday afternoons I used to go for a walk with my mother. From the dusk of the hallway, we stepped at once into the brightness of the day. The passers-by, bathed in melting gold, had their eyes half closed against the glare, as if they were drenched with honey. Upper lips were drawn back, exposing the teeth. Everyone in this golden day wore that grimace of heat—as if the sun had forced his worshipers to wear identical masks of gold. The old and the young, women and children, greeted each other with these masks, painted on their faces with thick gold paint; they smiled at each other's pagan faces—the barbaric smiles of Bacchus.

Market Square was empty and white-hot, swept by hot winds like a biblical desert. The thorny acacias, growing in this emptiness, looked with their bright leaves like the trees on old tapestries. Although there was no breath of wind, they rustled their foliage in a theatrical gesture, as if wanting to display the elegance of the silver lining of their leaves that resembled the fox-fur lining of a nobleman's coat. The old houses, worn smooth by the winds of innumerable days, played tricks with the reflections of the atmosphere, with echoes and memories of colors scattered in the depth of the cloudless sky. It seemed as if whole generations of summer days, like patient stonemasons cleaning the mildewed plaster from old façades, had removed the deceptive varnish, revealing more and more clearly the true face of the houses, the features that fate had given them and life had shaped for them from the inside. Now the windows, blinded by the glare of the empty square, had fallen asleep; the balconies declared their emptiness to heaven; the open doorways smelt of coolness and wine.

A bunch of ragamuffins, sheltering in a corner of the square from the flaming broom of the heat, beleaguered a piece of wall, throwing buttons and coins at it over and over again, as if wishing to read in the horoscope of those metal discs the real secret written in the hieroglyphics of cracks and scratched lines. Apart from them, the square was deserted. One expected that, any minute, the Samaritan's donkey, led by the bridle, would stop in front of the wine merchant's vaulted doorway and that two servants would carefully ease a sick man from the red-hot saddle and carry him slowly up the cool stairs to the floor above, already redolent of the Sabbath.

Thus my mother and I ambled along the two sunny sides of Market Square, guiding our broken shadows along the houses as over a keyboard. Under our soft steps the squares of the paving stones slowly filed past—some the pale pink of human skin, some golden, some blue-gray, all flat, warm and velvety in the sun, like sundials, trodden to the point of obliteration, into blessed nothingness.

And finally on the corner of Stryjska Street we passed within the shadow of the chemist's shop. A large jar of raspberry juice in the wide window symbolized the coolness of balms which can relieve all kinds of pain. After we passed a few more houses, the street ceased to maintain any pretense of urbanity, like a man returning to his little village who, piece by piece, strips off his Sunday best, slowly changing back into a peasant as he gets closer to his home.

The suburban houses were sinking, windows and all, into the exuberant tangle of blossom in their little gardens. Overlooked by the light of day, weeds and wild flowers of all kinds luxuriated quietly, glad of the interval for dreams beyond the margin of time on the borders of an endless day. An enormous sunflower, lifted on a powerful stem and suffering from hypertrophy, clad in the yellow mourning of the last sorrowful days of its life, bent under the weight of its monstrous girth. But the naïve, suburban bluebells and unpretentious dimity flowers stood helpless in their starched pink and white shifts, indifferent to the sunflower's tragedy.

2

A tangled thicket of grasses, weeds, and thistles crackled in the fire of the afternoon. The sleeping garden was resonant with flies. The golden field of stubble shouted in the sun like a tawny cloud of locusts; in the thick rain of fire the crickets screamed; seed pods exploded softly like grasshoppers.

And over by the fence the sheepskin of grass lifted in

a hump, as if the garden had turned over in its sleep, its broad, peasant back rising and falling as it breathed on the stillness of the earth. There the untidy, feminine ripeness of August had expanded into enormous, impenetrable clumps of burdocks spreading their sheets of leafy tin, their luxuriant tongues of fleshy greenery. There, those protuberant bur clumps spread themselves, like resting peasant women, half-enveloped in their own swirling skirts. There, the garden offered free of charge the cheapest fruits of wild lilac, the heady aquavit of mint and all kinds of August trash. But on the other side of the fence, behind that jungle of summer in which the stupidity of weeds reigned unchecked, there was a rubbish heap on which thistles grew in wild profusion. No one knew that there, on that refuse dump, the month of August had chosen to hold that year its pagan orgies. There, pushed against the fence and hidden by the elders, stood the bed of the half-wit girl, Touya, as we all called her. On a heap of discarded junk of old saucepans, abandoned single shoes, and chunks of plaster, stood a bed, painted green, propped up on two bricks where one leg was missing.

The air over that midden, wild with the heat, cut through by the lightning of shiny horseflies, driven mad by the sun, crackled, as if filled with invisible rattles, exciting one to frenzy.

Touya sits hunched up among the yellow bedding and odd rags, her large head covered by a mop of tangled black hair. Her face works like the bellows of an accordion. Every now and then a sorrowful grimace folds it into a thousand vertical pleats, but astonishment soon straightens it out again, ironing out the folds, revealing the chinks of small eyes and damp gums with yellow teeth under snoutlike, fleshy lips. Hours pass, filled with heat and boredom; Touya chatters in a monotone, dozes, mumbles softly, and coughs. Her immobile frame is covered by a thick cloak of flies. But suddenly the whole heap of dirty rags begins to move, as if stirred by the scratching of a litter of newborn rats. The flies wake up in fright and rise in a huge, furiously buzzing cloud, filled with colored light reflected from the sun. And while the rags slip to the ground and spread out over the rubbish heap, like frightened rats, a form emerges and reveals itself: the dark half-naked idiot girl rises slowly to her feet and stands like a pagan idol, on short childish legs; her neck swells with anger, and from her face, red with fury, on which the arabesques of bulging veins stand out as in a primitive painting, comes forth a hoarse animal scream, originating deep in the lungs hidden in that half-animal, half-divine breast. The sun-dried thistles shout, the plantains swell and boast their shameless flesh, the weeds salivate with glistening poison, and the half-wit girl, hoarse with shouting, convulsed with madness, presses her fleshy belly in an access of lust against the trunk of an elder, which groans softly under the insistent pressure of that libidinous passion, incited by the whole ghastly chorus to hideous unnatural fertility.

Touya's mother Maria hired herself to housewives to scrub floors. She was a small saffron-yellow woman, and it was with saffron that she wiped the floors, the deal tables, the benches, and the banisters which she had scrubbed in the homes of the poor.

Once Adela took me to the old woman's house. It was early in the morning when we entered the small blue-walled room, with its mud floor, lying in a patch of bright yellow sunlight in the still of the morning broken only by the frighteningly loud ticking of a cottage clock on the wall. In a straw-filled chest lay the foolish Maria, white as a wafer and motionless like a glove from which a hand had been withdrawn. And, as if taking advantage of her sleep, the silence talked, the yellow, bright, evil silence delivered its monologue, argued, and loudly spoke its vulgar maniacal soliloquy. Maria's time—the time imprisoned in her soul—had left her and—terribly real—filled the room, vociferous and hellish in the bright silence of the morning, rising from the noisy mill of the clock like a cloud of bad flour, powdery flour, the stupid flour of madmen.

3

In one of those cottages, surrounded by brown railings and submerged in the lush green of its garden, lived Aunt Agatha. Coming through the garden to visit her, we passed numerous colored glass balls stuck on flimsy poles. In these pink, green, and violet balls were enclosed bright shining worlds, like the ideally happy pictures contained in the peerless perfection of soap bubbles.

In the gloom of the hall, with its old lithographs, rotten with mildew and blind with age, we rediscovered a well-known smell. In that old familiar smell was contained a marvelously simple synthesis of the life of those people, the distillation of their race, the quality of their blood, and the secret of their fate, imperceptibly mixed day by day with the passage of their own, private, time. The old, wise door, the silent witness of the entries and exits of mother, daughters, sons, whose dark sighs accompanied the comings and goings of those people, now opened noiselessly like the door of a wardrobe, and we stepped into their life. They were sitting as if in the shadow of their own destiny and did not fight against it; with their first, clumsy gestures they revealed their secret to us. Besides, were we not related to them by blood and by fate?

The room was dark and velvety from the royal blue wallpaper with its gold pattern, but even here the echo of the flaming day shimmered brassily on the picture frames, on door knobs and gilded borders, although it came through the filter of the dense greenery of the garden. From her chair against the wall, Aunt Agatha rose to greet us, tall and ample, her round white flesh blotchy with the rust of freckles. We sat down beside them, as on the verge of their lives, rather embarrassed by their defenseless surrender to us, and we drank water with rose syrup, a wonderful drink in which I found the deepest essence of that hot Saturday.

My aunt was complaining. It was the principal burden of her conversation, the voice of that white and fertile flesh, floating as it were outside the boundaries of her person, held only loosely in the fetters of individual form, and, despite those fetters, ready to multiply, to scatter, branch out, and divide into a family. It was an almost self-propagating fertility, a femininity without rein, morbidly expansive.

It seemed as if the very whiff of masculinity, the smell of tobacco smoke, or a bachelor's joke, would spark off this feverish feminity and entice it to a lascivious virgin birth. And in fact, all her complaints about her husband or her servants, all her worries about the children were only the caprices of her incompletely satisfied fertility, a logical extension of the rude, angry, lachrymose coquetry with which, to no purpose, she plagued her husband. Uncle Mark, small and hunched, with a face fallow of sex, sat in his gray bankruptcy, reconciled to his fate, in the shadow of a limitless contempt in which he seemed only to relax. His gray eyes reflected the distant glow of the garden, spreading in the window.

Sometimes he tried with a feeble gesture to raise an objection, to resist, but the wave of self-sufficient femininity hurled aside that unimportant gesture, triumphantly passed him by, and drowned the feeble stirrings of male assertiveness under its broad flood.

There was something tragic in that immoderate fertility; the misery of a creature fighting on the borders of nothingness and death, the heroism of womanhood triumphing by fertility over the shortcomings of nature, over the insufficiency of the male. But their offspring showed justification for that panic of maternity, of a passion for childbearing which became exhausted in ill-starred pregnancies, in an ephemeral generation of phantoms without blood or face.

Lucy, the second eldest, now entered the room, her head overdeveloped for her childlike, plump body, her flesh white and delicate. She stretched out to me a small doll-like hand, a hand in bud, and blushed all over her face like a peony. Unhappy because of her blushes, which shamelessly revealed the secrets of menstruation, she closed her eyes and reddened even more deeply under the touch of the most indifferent question, for she saw in each a secret allusion to her most sensitive maidenhood.

Emil, the eldest of the cousins, with a fair mustache in a face from which life seemed to have washed away all expression, was walking up and down the room, his hands in the pockets of his voluminous trousers.

His elegant, expensive clothes bore the imprint of the exotic countries he had visited. His pale flabby face seemed from day to day to lose its outline, to become a white blank wall with a pale network of veins, like lines on an old map occasionally stirred by the fading memories of a stormy and wasted life.

He was a master of card tricks, he smoked long, noble pipes, and he smelled strangely of distant lands. With his gaze wandering over old memories, he told curious stories, which at some point would suddenly stop, disintegrate, and blow away.

My eyes followed him nostalgically, and I wished he would notice me and liberate me from the tortures of boredom. And indeed, it seemed as if he gave me a wink before going into an adjoining room and I followed him there. He was sitting on a small low sofa, his crossed knees almost level with his head, which was bald like a billiard ball. It seemed as if it were only his clothes that had been thrown, crumpled and empty, over a chair. His face seemed like the breath of a face—a smudge which an unknown passer-by had left in the air. In his white, blue-enameled hands he was holding a wallet and looking at something in it.

From the mist of his face, the protruding white of a pale eye emerged with difficulty, enticing me with a wink. I felt an irresistible sympathy for Emil.

He took me between his knees and, shuffling some photographs in front of my eyes as if they were a pack of cards, he showed me naked women and boys in strange positions. I stood leaning against him looking at those delicate human bodies with distant, unseeing eyes, when all of a sudden the fluid of an obscure excitement with which the air seemed charged, reached me and pierced me with a shiver of uneasiness, a wave of sudden comprehension. But meanwhile that ghost of a smile which had appeared under Emil's soft and beautiful mustache, the seed of desire which had shown in a pulsating vein on his temple, the tenseness which for a moment had kept his features concentrated, all fell away again and his face receded into indifference and became absent and finally faded away altogether.

Visitation

1

Already for some time our town had been sinking into the perpetual grayness of dusk, had become affected at the edges by a rash of shadows, by fluffy mildew, and by moss the dull color of iron.

Hardly was it freed from the brown smoke and the mists of the morning, than the day turned into a lowering amber afternoon, became for a brief moment transparent, taking the golden color of ale, only to ascend under the multiple fantastic domes of vast, color-filled nights.

We lived on Market Square, in one of those dark houses with empty blind looks, so difficult to distinguish one from the other.

This gave endless possibilities for mistakes. For, once you had entered the wrong doorway and set foot on the wrong staircase, you were liable to find yourself in a real labyrinth of unfamiliar apartments and balconies, and unexpected doors opening onto strange empty court-yards, and you forgot the initial object of the expedition, only to recall it days later after numerous strange and complicated adventures, on regaining the family home in the gray light of dawn.

Full of large wardrobes, vast sofas, faded mirrors, and cheap artificial palms, our apartment sank deeper and deeper into a state of neglect owing to the indolence of my mother, who spent most of her time in the shop, and the carelessness of slim-legged Adela, who, without anyone to supervise her, spent her days in front of a mirror, endlessly making up and leaving everywhere tufts of combed-out hair, brushes, odd slippers, and discarded corsets.

No one ever knew exactly how many rooms we had in our apartment, because no one ever remembered how many of them were let to strangers. Often one would by chance open the door to one of these forgotten rooms and find it empty; the lodger had moved out a long time ago. In the drawers, untouched for months, one would make unexpected discoveries.

In the downstairs rooms lived the shop assistants and sometimes during the night we were awakened by their nightmares. In winter it would be still deep night when Father went down to these cold and dark rooms, the light of his candle scattering flocks of shadows so that they fled sideways along the floor and up the walls; his task to wake the snoring men from their stone-hard sleep.

In the light of the candle, which Father left with them, they unwound themselves lazily from the dirty bedding, then, sitting on the edge of their beds, stuck out their bare and ugly feet and, with socks in their hands, abandoned themselves for a moment to the delights of yawning—a yawning crossing the borders of sensuous pleasure, leading to a painful cramp of the palate, almost to nausea.

In the corners, large cockroaches sat immobile, hideously enlarged by their own shadows which the burning candle imposed on them and which remained attached to their flat, headless bodies when they suddenly ran off with weird, spiderlike movements.

At that time, my father's health began to fail. Even in the first weeks of this early winter, he would spend whole days in bed, surrounded by bottles of medicine and boxes of pills, and ledgers brought up to him from the shop. The bitter smell of illness settled like a rug in the room and the arabesques on the wallpaper loomed darker.

In the evenings, when Mother returned from the shop, Father was often excited and inclined to argue.

As he reproached her for inaccuracies in the accounts his cheeks became flushed and he became almost insane with anger. I remember more than once waking in the middle of the night to see him in his nightshirt, running in his bare feet up and down the leather sofa to demonstrate his irritation to my baffled mother.

On other days he was calm and composed, completely absorbed in the account books, lost in a maze of complicated calculations.

I can still see him in the light of the smoking lamp, crouched among his pillows under the large carved headboard of the bed, swaying backward and forward in silent meditation, his head making an enormous shadow on the wall.

From time to time, he raised his eyes from the ledgers as if to come up for air, opened his mouth, smacked his lips with distaste as if his tongue were dry and bitter, and looked around helplessly, as if searching for something.

It then sometimes happened that he quietly got out of bed and ran to the corner of the room where an intimate instrument hung on the wall. It was a kind of hourglass-shaped water jar marked in ounces and filled with a dark fluid. My father attached himself to it with a long rubber hose as if with a gnarled, aching navel cord, and thus connected with the miserable apparatus, he became tense with concentration, his eyes darkened, and an expression of suffering, or perhaps of forbidden pleasure, spread over his pale face.

Then again came days of quiet, concentrated work, interrupted by lonely monologues. While he sat there in the light of the lamp among the pillows of the large bed, and the room grew enormous as the shadows above the lampshade merged with the deep city night beyond the windows, he felt, without looking, how the pullulating jungle of wallpaper, filled with whispers, lisping and hissing, closed in around him. He heard, without looking, a conspiracy of knowingly winking hidden eyes, of alert ears opening up among the flowers on the wall, of dark, smiling mouths.

He then pretended to become even more engrossed in his work, adding and calculating, trying not to betray the anger which rose in him and overcoming the temptation to throw himself blindly forward with a sudden shout to grab fistfuls of those curly arabesques, or of those sheaves of eyes and ears which swarmed out from the night and grew and multiplied, sprouting, with ever-new ghostlike shoots and branches, from the womb of darkness. And he calmed down only when, in the morning with the ebb of night, the wallpaper wilted, shed its leaves and petals and thinned down autumnally, letting in the distant dawn.

Then, among the twittering of wallpaper birds in the yellow wintry dawn, he would fall, for a few hours, into a heavy black sleep.

For days, even for weeks, while he seemed to be engrossed in the complicated current accounts—his thoughts had been secretly plumbing the depths of his own entrails. He would hold his breath and listen. And when his gaze returned, pale and troubled, from that labyrinth, he calmed it with a smile. He did not wish to believe those assumptions and suggestions which oppressed him, and rejected them as absurd.

In daytime, these were more like arguments and persuasions; long monotonous reasonings, conducted half-aloud and with humorous interludes of teasing and banter. But at night these voices rose with greater passion. The demands were made more clearly and more loudly, and we heard him talk to God, as if begging for something or fighting against someone who made insistent claims and issued orders.

Until one night that voice rose threateningly and irresistibly, demanding that he should bear witness to it with his mouth and with his entrails. And we heard the spirit enter into him as he rose from his bed, tall and growing in prophetic anger, choking with brash words that he emitted like a machine gun. We heard the din of battle and Father's groans, the groans of a titan with a broken hip, but still capable of wrath.

I have never seen an Old Testament prophet, but at the sight of this man stricken by God's fire, sitting clumsily on an enormous china chamberpot behind a windmill of arms, a screen of desperate wrigglings over which there towered his voice, grown unfamiliar and hard, I understood the divine anger of saintly men.

It was a dialogue as grim as the language of thunder. The jerkings of his arms cut the sky into pieces, and in the cracks there appeared the face of Jehovah swollen with anger and spitting out curses. Without looking, I saw him, the terrible Demiurge, as, resting on darkness as on Sinai, propping his powerful palms on the pelmet of the curtains, he pressed his enormous face against the upper panes of the window which flattened horribly his large fleshy nose.

I heard my father's voice during the intermissions in these prophetic tirades. I heard the windows shake from the powerful growl of the swollen lips, mixed with the explosions of entreaties, laments, and threats uttered by Father.

Sometimes the voices quietened down and grumbled softly, like the nightly chatter of wind in a chimney, then again they exploded with a large, tumultuous noise, in a storm of sobs mixed with curses. Suddenly the window opened with a dark yawn and a sheet of darkness wafted across the room.

In a flash of lightning I could see my father, his night-shirt unbuttoned, as, cursing terribly, he emptied with a masterful gesture the contents of the chamberpot into the darkness below.

2

My father was slowly fading, wilting before our eyes.

Hunched among the enormous pillows, his gray hair standing wildly on end, he talked to himself in undertones, engrossed in some complicated private business. It seemed as if his personality had split into a number of opposing and quarreling selves; he argued loudly with himself, persuading forcibly and passionately, pleading and begging; then again he seemed to be presiding over a meeting of many interested parties whose views he tried to reconcile with a great show of energy and conviction. But every time these noisy meetings, during which tempers would rise violently, dissolved into curses, execrations, maledictions, and insults.

Then came a period of appeasement, of an interior calm, a blessed serenity of spirit. Again the great ledgers were spread on the bed, on the table, on the floor, and an almost monastic calm reigned in the light of the lamp, over the white bedding, over my father's gray, bowed head.

But when Mother returned late at night from the shop, Father became animated, called her and showed her with great pride the wonderful colored decals with which he had laboriously adorned the pages of the main ledger.

About that time we noticed that Father began to shrink from day to day, like a nut drying inside the shell.

This shrinking was not accompanied by any loss of strength. On the contrary: there seemed to be an improvement in his general state of health, in his humor, and in his mobility.

Now he often laughed loudly and gaily; sometimes he was almost overcome with laughter; at others, he would knock on the side of the bed and answer himself: "Come in," in various tones, for hours on end. From time to time, he scrambled down from the bed, climbed on top of the wardrobe, and, crouching under the ceiling, sorted out old dust-covered odds and ends.

Sometimes he put two chairs back to back and taking his weight on them, swung his legs backward and forward, looking with shining eyes for an expression of admiration and encouragement in our faces. It seemed as if he had become completely reconciled with God. Sometimes at night, the face of the bearded Demiurge would appear at the bedroom window, bathed in the dark purple glare of Bengal fire, but it only looked for a moment benevolently on my sleeping father whose melodious snoring seemed to wander far into the unknown regions of the world of sleep.

During the long twilight afternoons of this winter, my father would spend hours rummaging in corners full of old junk, as if he were feverishly searching for something.

And sometimes at dinnertime, when we had all taken our places at the table, Father would be missing. On such occasions, Mother had to call "Jacob!" over and over again and knock her spoon against the table before he emerged from inside a wardrobe, covered with dust and cobwebs, his eyes vacant, his mind on some complicated matter known only to himself which absorbed him completely.

Occasionally he climbed on a pelmet and froze into immobility, a counterpart to the large stuffed vulture which hung on the wall opposite. In this crouching pose, with misty eyes and a sly smile on his lips, he remained for long periods without moving, except to flap his arms like wings and crow like a cock whenever anybody entered the room.

We ceased to pay attention to these oddities in which Father became daily more and more involved. Almost completely rid of bodily needs, not taking any nourishment for weeks, he plunged deeper every day into some strange and complex affairs that were beyond our understanding. To all our persuasions and our entreaties, he answered in fragments of his interior monologue, which nothing from the outside could disturb. Constantly absorbed, morbidly excited, with flushes on his dry cheeks he did not notice us or even hear us any more.

We became used to his harmless presence, to his soft babbling, and that childlike self-absorbed twittering, which sounded as if they came from the margin of our own time. During that period he used to disappear for many days into some distant corner of the house and it was difficult to locate him.

Gradually these disappearances ceased to make any impression on us, we became used to them and when, after many days, Father reappeared a few inches shorter and much thinner, we did not stop to think about it. We did not count him as one of us any more, so very remote had he become from everything that was human and real. Knot by knot, he loosened himself from us; point by point, he gave up the ties joining him to the human community.

What still remained of him—the small shroud of his body and the handful of nonsensical oddities—would finally disappear one day, as unremarked as the gray heap of rubbish swept into a corner, waiting to be taken by Adela to the rubbish dump.

Birds

Came the yellow days of winter, filled with boredom. The rust-colored earth was covered with a threadbare, meager tablecloth of snow full of holes. There was not enough of it for some of the roofs and so they stood there, black and brown, shingle and thatch, arks containing the sooty expanses of attics—coal-black cathedrals, bristling with ribs of rafters, beams, and spars—the dark lungs of winter winds. Each dawn revealed new chimney stacks and chimney pots which had emerged during the hours of darkness, blown up by the night winds: the black pipes of a devil's organ. The chimney sweeps could not get rid of the crows which in the evening covered the branches of the trees around the church with living black leaves, then took off, fluttering, and came back, each clinging to its own place on its own branch, only to fly away at dawn in large flocks, like gusts of soot, flakes of dirt, undulating and fantastic, blackening with their insistent crowing the musty-yellow streaks of light. The days hardened with cold and boredom like last year's loaves of bread. One began to cut them with blunt knives without appetite, with a lazy indifference.

Father had stopped going out. He banked up the stoves, studied the ever-elusive essence of fire, experienced the salty, metallic taste and the smoky smell of wintry flames, the cool caresses of salamanders that licked the shiny soot in the throat of the chimney. He applied himself lovingly at that time to all manner of small repairs in the upper regions of the rooms. At all hours of the day one could see him crouched on top of a ladder, working at something under the ceiling, at the cornices over the tall windows, at the counterweights and chains of the hanging lamps. Following the custom of house painters, he used a pair of steps as enormous stilts and he felt perfectly happy in that bird's eye perspective close to the sky, leaves and birds painted on the ceiling. He grew more and more remote from practical affairs. When my mother, worried and unhappy about his condition, tried to draw him into a conversation about business, about the payments due at the end of the month, he listened to her absent-mindedly, anxiety showing in his abstracted look. Sometimes he stopped her with a warning gesture of the hand in order to run to a corner of the room, put his ear to a crack in the floor and, by lifting the index fingers of both hands, emphasize the gravity of the investigation, and begin to listen intently. At that time we did not yet understand the sad origin of these eccentricities, the deplorable complex which had been maturing in him.

Mother had no influence over him, but he gave a lot of respectful attention to Adela. The cleaning of his room was to him a great and important ceremony, of which he always arranged to be a witness, watching all Adela's movements with a mixture of apprehension and pleasurable excitement. He ascribed to all her functions a deeper, symbolic meaning. When, with young firm gestures, the girl pushed a long-handled broom along the floor, Father could hardly bear it. Tears would stream from his eyes, silent laughter transformed his face, and his body was shaken by spasms of delight. He was ticklish to the point of madness. It was enough for Adela to waggle her fingers at him to imitate tickling, for him to rush through all the rooms in a wild panic, banging the doors after him, to fall at last flat on the bed in the farthest room and wriggle in convulsions of laughter, imagining the tickling which he found irresistible. Because of this, Adela's power over Father was almost limitless.

At that time we noticed for the first time Father's passionate interest in animals. To begin with, it was the passion of the huntsman and the artist rolled into one. It was also perhaps a deeper, biological sympathy of one creature for kindred, yet different, forms of life, a kind of experimenting in the unexplored regions of existence. Only at a later stage did matters take that uncanny, complicated, essentially sinful and unnatural turn, which it is better not to bring into the light of day.

But it all began with the hatching out of birds' eggs.

With a great outlay of effort and money, Father imported from Hamburg, or Holland, or from zoological stations in Africa, birds' eggs on which he set enormous brood hens from Belgium. It was a process which fascinated me as well—this hatching out of the chicks, which were real anomalies of shape and color. It was difficult to anticipate—in these monsters with enormous, fantastic beaks which they opened wide immediately after birth, hissing greedily to show the backs of their throats, in these lizards with frail, naked bodies of hunchbacks—the future peacocks, pheasants, grouse, or condors. Placed in cotton wool, in baskets, this dragon brood lifted blind, walleyed heads on thin necks, croaking voicelessly from their dumb throats. My father would walk along the shelves, dressed in a green baize apron, like a gardener in a hothouse of cacti, and conjure up from nothingness these blind bubbles, pulsating with life, these impotent bellies receiving the outside world only in the form of food, these growths on the surface of life, climbing blindfold toward the light. A few weeks later, when these blind buds of matter burst open, the rooms were filled with the bright chatter and scintillating chirruping of their new inhabitants. The birds perched on the curtain pelmets, on the tops of wardrobes; they nestled in the tangle of tin branches and the metal scrolls of the hanging lamps.

While Father pored over his large ornithological textbooks and studied their colored plates, these feathery phantasms seemed to rise from the pages and fill the rooms with colors, with splashes of crimson, strips of sapphire, verdigris, and silver. At feeding time they formed a motley, undulating bed on the floor, a living carpet which at the intrusion of a stranger would fall apart, scatter into fragments, flutter in the air, and finally settle high under the ceilings. I remember in particular a certain condor, an enormous bird with a featherless neck, its face wrinkled and knobbly. It was an emaciated ascetic, a Buddhist lama, full of imperturbable dignity in its behavior, guided by the rigid ceremonial of its great species. When it sat facing my father, motionless in the monumental position of ageless Egyptian idols, its eye covered with a whitish cataract which it pulled down sideways over its pupil to shut itself up completely in the contemplation of its dignified solitude—it seemed, with its stony profile, like an older brother of my father's. Its body and muscles seemed to be made of the same material, it had the same hard, wrinkled skin, the same desiccated bony face, the same horny, deep eye sockets. Even the hands, strong in the joints, my father's long thick hands with their rounded nails, had their counterpart in the condor's claws. I could not resist the impression, when looking at the sleeping condor, that I was in the presence of a mummy—a dried-out, shrunken mummy of my father. I believe that even my mother noticed this strange resemblance, although we never discussed the subject. It is significant that the condor used my father's chamberpot.

Not content with the hatching out of more and more new specimens, my father arranged the marriages of birds in the attic, he sent out matchmakers, he tied up eager attractive brides in the holes and crannies under the roof, and soon the roof of our house, an enormous double-ridged shingle roof, became a real birds' hostel, a Noah's ark to which all kinds of feathery creatures flew from far afield. Long after the liquidation of the birds' paradise, this tradition persisted in the avian world and during the period of spring migration our roof was besieged by whole flocks of cranes, pelicans, peacocks, and sundry other birds. However, after a short period of splendor, the whole undertaking took a sorry turn.

It soon became necessary to move my father to two rooms at the top of the house which had served as storage rooms. We could hear from there, at dawn, the mixed clangor of birds' voices. The wooden walls of the attic rooms, helped by the resonance of the empty space under the gables, sounded with the roar, the flutterings, the crowing, the gurgling, the mating cries. For a few weeks Father was lost to view. He only rarely came down to the apartment and, when he did, we noticed that he seemed to have shrunk, to have become smaller and thinner. Occasionally forgetting himself, he would rise from his chair at table, wave his arms as if they were wings, and emit a long-drawn-out bird's call while his eyes misted over. Then, rather embarrassed, he would join us in laughing it off and try to turn the whole incident into a joke.

One day, during spring cleaning, Adela suddenly appeared in Father's bird kingdom. Stopping in the doorway, she wrung her hands at the fetid smell that filled the room, the heaps of droppings covering the floor, the tables, and the chairs. Without hesitation, she flung open a window and, with the help of a long broom, she prodded the whole mass of birds into life. A fiendish cloud of feathers and wings arose screaming, and Adela, like a furious maenad protected by the whirlwind of her thyrsus, danced the dance of destruction. My father, waving his arms in panic, tried to lift himself into the air with his feathered flock. Slowly the winged cloud thinned until at last Adela remained on the battlefield, exhausted and out of breath, along with my father, who now, adopting a worried hangdog expression, was ready to accept complete defeat.

A moment later, my father came downstairs—a broken man, an exiled king who had lost his throne and his kingdom.

Tailors' Dummies

The affair of the birds was the last colorful and splendid counteroffensive of fantasy which my father, that incorrigible improviser, that fencing master of imagination, had led against the trenches and defenseworks of a sterile and empty winter. Only now do I understand the lonely hero who alone had waged war against the fathomless, elemental boredom that strangled the city. Without any support, without recognition on our part, that strangest of men was defending the lost cause of poetry. He was like a magic mill, into the hoppers of which the bran of empty hours was poured, to re-emerge flowering in all the colors and scents of Oriental spices. But, used to the splendid showmanship of that metaphysical conjurer, we were inclined to underrate the value of his sovereign magic, which saved us from the lethargy of empty days and nights.

Adela was not rebuked for her thoughtless and brutal vandalism. On the contrary, we felt a vile satisfaction, a

aggressive language

51

disgraceful pleasure that Father's exuberance had been curbed, for although we had enjoyed it to the full, we later ignominiously denied all responsibility for it. Perhaps in our treachery there was secret approval of the victorious Adela to whom we dimly ascribed some commission and assignment from forces of a higher order. Betrayed by us all, Father retreated without a fight from the scenes of his recent glory. Without crossing swords, he surrendered to the enemy the kingdom of his former splendor. A voluntary exile, he took himself off to an empty room at the end of the passage and there immured himself in solitude.

We forgot him.

We were beset again from all sides by the mournful grayness of the city which crept through the windows with the dark rash of dawn, with the mushroom growth of dusk, developing into the shaggy fur of long winter nights. The wallpaper of the rooms, blissfully unconstrained in those former days and accessible to the multicolored flights of the birds, closed in on itself and hardened, becoming engrossed in the monotony of bitter monologues.

The chandeliers blackened and wilted like old thistles; now they hung dejected and ill-tempered, their glass pendants ringing softly whenever anybody groped their way through the dimly lit room. In vain did Adela put colored candles in all the holders; they were a poor substitute for, a pale reflection of, those splendid illuminations which had so recently enlivened these hanging gardens. Oh, what a twittering had been there, what swift and fantastic flights cutting the air into packs of magic cards, sprinkling thick flakes of azure, of peacock and parrot green, of metallic sparkle, drawing lines and flourishes in the air, displaying colored fans which remained suspended, long after flight, in the shimmering atmosphere. Even now, in the depth of the grayness, echoes and memories of brightness were hidden but nobody caught them, no clarinet drilled the troubled air.

Those weeks passed under the sign of a strange drowsiness.

Beds unmade for days on end, piled high with bedding crumpled and disordered from the weight of dreams, stood like deep boats waiting to sail into the dank and confusing labyrinths of some dark starless Venice. In the bleakness of dawn, Adela brought us coffee. Lazily we started dressing in the cold rooms, in the light of a single candle reflected many times in black windowpanes. The mornings were full of aimless bustle, of prolonged searches in endless drawers and cupboards. The clacking of Adela's slippers could be heard all over the apartment. The shop assistants lit the lanterns, took the large shop keys which mother handed them and went out into the thick swirling darkness. Mother could not come to terms with her dressing. The candles burned smaller in the candlesticks. Adela disappeared somewhere into the farthest rooms or into the attic where she hung the washing. She was deaf to our calling. A newly lit, dirty, bleak fire in the stove licked at the cold, shiny growth of soot in the throat of the chimney. The candle died out, and the room filled with gloom. With our heads on the tablecloth, among the remains of breakfast, we fell asleep, still half-dressed. Lying face downward on the furry lap of darkness, we sailed in its regular breathing into the starless nothingness. We were awakened by Adela's noisy tidying up. Mother could not cope with her dressing. Before she had finished doing her hair, the shop assistants were back for lunch. The half-light in the market place was now the color of golden smoke. For a moment it looked as if out of that smoke-colored honey, that opaque amber, a most beautiful afternoon would unfold. But the happy moment passed, the amalgam of dawn withered, the swelling fermentation of the day, almost completed, receded again into a helpless grayness. We assembled again around the table, the shop assistants rubbed their hands, red from the cold, and the prose of their conversation suddenly revealed a full-grown day, a gray and empty Tuesday, a day without tradition and without a face. But it was only when a dish appeared on the table containing two large fish in jelly lying side by side, head-to-tail, like a sign of the zodiac, that we recognized in them the coat of arms of that day, the calendar emblem of the nameless Tuesday: we shared it out quickly among ourselves, thankful that the day had at last achieved an identity.

The shop assistants ate with unction, with the seriousness due to a calendar feast. The smell of pepper filled the room. And when they had used pieces of bread to wipe up the remains of the jelly from their plates, pondering in silence on the heraldry of the following days of the week, and nothing remained on the serving dish but the fishheads with their boiled-out eyes, we all felt that by a communal effort we had conquered the day and that what remained of it did not matter.

And, in fact, Adela made short work of the rest of the day, now surrendered to her mercies. Amid the clatter of saucepans and splashing of cold water, she was energetically liquidating the few hours remaining until dusk, while Mother slept on the sofa. Meanwhile, in the dining room the scene was being set for the evening. Polda and

Pauline, the seamstresses, spread themselves out there with the props of their trade. Carried on their shoulders, a silent immobile lady had entered the room, a lady of oakum and canvas, with a black wooden knob instead of a head. But when stood in the corner, between the door and the stove, that silent woman became mistress of the situation. Standing motionless in her corner, she supervised the girls' advances and wooings as they knelt before her, fittings fragments of a dress marked with white basting thread. They waited with attention and patience on the silent idol, which was difficult to please. That moloch was inexorable as only a female moloch can be, and sent them back to work again and again, and they, thin and spindly, like wooden spools from which thread is unwound and as mobile, manipulated with deft fingers the piles of silk and wool, cut with noisy scissors into its colorful mass, whirred the sewing machine, treading its pedal with one cheap patent-leathered foot, while around them there grew a heap of cuttings, of motley rags and pieces, like husks and chaff spat out by two fussy and prodigal parrots. The curved jaws of the scissors tapped open like the beaks of those exotic birds.

The girls trod absent-mindedly on the bright shreds of material, wading carelessly in the rubbish of a possible carnival, in the storeroom for some great unrealized masquerade. They disentangled themselves with nervous giggles from the trimmings, their eyes laughed into the mirrors. Their hearts, the quick magic of their fingers, were not in the boring dresses which remained on the table, but in the thousand scraps, the frivolous and fickle trimmings, with the colorful fantastic snowstorm with which they could smother the whole city.

Suddenly they felt hot and opened the window to see,

in the frustration of their solitude, in their hunger for new faces, at least one nameless face pressed against the pane. They fanned their flushed cheeks with the winter night air in which the curtains billowed—they uncovered their burning décolletés, full of hatred and rivalry for one another, ready to fight for any Pierrot whom the dark breezes of night might blow in through the window. Ah! how little did they demand from reality! They had everything within themselves, they had a surfeit of everything in themselves. Ah! they would be content with a sawdust Pierrot with the long-awaited word to act as the cue for their well-rehearsed roles, so that they could at last speak the lines, full of a sweet and terrible bitterness, that crowded to their lips exciting them violently, like some novel devoured at night, while the tears streamed down their cheeks.

During one of his nightly wanderings about the apartment, undertaken in Adela's absence, my father stumbled upon such a quiet evening sewing session. For a moment he stood in the dark door of the adjoining room, a lamp in his hand, enchanted by the scene of feverish activity, by the blushes—that synthesis of face powder, red tissue paper, and atropine—to which the winter night, breathing on the waving window curtains, acted as a significant backdrop. Putting on his glasses, he stepped quickly up to the girls and walked twice around them, letting fall on them the light of the lamp he was carrying. The draft from the open door lifted the curtains, the girls let themselves be admired, twisting their hips; the enamel of their eyes glinted like the shiny leather of their shoes and the buckles of their garters, showing from under their skirts lifted by the wind; the scraps began to scamper across the floor like rats toward the half-closed door of the dark room, and my father gazed attentively at the panting girls, whispering softly: *"Genus avium* . . . If I am not mistaken, Scansores or Psittacus . . . very remarkable, very remarkable indeed."

This accidental encounter was the beginning of a whole series of meetings, in the course of which my father succeeded in charming both of the young ladies with the magnetism of his strange personality. In return for his witty and elegant conversation, which filled the emptiness of their evenings, the girls permitted the ardent ornithologist to study the structure of their thin and ordinary little bodies. This took place while the conversation was in progress and was done with a seriousness and grace which insured that even the more risky points of these researches remained completely unequivocal. Pulling Pauline's stocking down from her knee and studying with enraptured eyes the precise and noble structure of the joint, my father would say:

"How delightful and happy is the form of existence which you ladies have chosen. How beautiful and simple is the truth which is revealed by your lives. And with what mastery, with what precision you are performing your task. If, forgetting the respect due to the Creator, I were to attempt a criticism of creation, I would say 'Less matter, more form!' Ah, what relief it would be for the world to lose some of its contents. More modesty in aspirations, more sobriety in claims, Gentlemen Demiurges, and the world would be more perfect!" my father exclaimed, while his hands released Pauline's white calf from the prison of her stocking.

At that moment Adela appeared in the open door of the dining room, the supper tray in her hands. This was the first meeting of the two enemy powers since the great battle. All of us who witnessed it felt a moment of terrible fear. We felt extremely uneasy at being present at the further humiliation of the sorely tried man. My father rose from his knees very disturbed, blushing more and more deeply in wave after wave of shame. But Adela found herself unexpectedly equal to the situation. She walked up to Father with a smile and flipped him on the nose. At that, Polda and Pauline clapped their hands, stamped their feet, and each grabbing one of Father's arms, began to dance with him around the table. Thus, because of the girls' good nature, the cloud of unpleasantness dispersed in general hilarity.

That was the beginning of a series of most interesting and most unusual lectures which my father, inspired by the charm of that small and innocent audience, delivered during the subsequent weeks of that early winter.

It is worth noting how, in contact with that strange man, all things reverted, as it were, to the roots of their existence, rebuilt their outward appearance anew from their metaphysical core, returned to the primary idea, in order to betray it at some point and to turn into the doubtful, risky and equivocal regions which we shall call for short the Regions of the Great Heresy. Our Heresiarch walked meanwhile like a mesmerist, infecting everything with his dangerous charm. Am I to call Pauline his victim? She became in those days his pupil and disciple, and at the same time a guinea pig for his experiments.)

Next I shall attempt to explain, with due care and without causing offense, this most heretical doctrine that held Father in its sway for many months to come and which during this time prompted all his actions.

Treatise on Tailors' Dummies, or
The Second Book of Genesis

"The Demiurge," said my father, "has had no monopoly of creation, for creation is the privilege of all spirits. Matter has been given infinite fertility, inexhaustible vitality, and, at the same time, a seductive power of temptation which invites us to create as well. In the depth of matter, indistinct smiles are shaped, tensions build up, attempts at form appear. The whole of matter pulsates with infinite possibilities that send dull shivers through it. Waiting for the life-giving breath of the spirit, it is endlessly in motion. It entices us with a thousand sweet, soft, round shapes which it blindly dreams up within itself.

"Deprived of all initiative, indulgently acquiescent, pliable like a woman, submissive to every impulse, it is a territory outside any law, open to all kinds of charlatans and dilettanti, a domain of abuses and of dubious demiurgical manipulations. Matter is the most passive and most defenseless essence in cosmos. Anyone can mold it and shape it; it obeys everybody. All attempts at organizing matter are transient and temporary, easy to reverse and to dissolve. There is no evil in reducing life to other and newer forms. Homicide is not a sin. It is sometimes a necessary violence on resistant and ossified forms of existence which have ceased to be amusing. In the interests of an important and fascinating experiment, it can even become meritorious. Here is the starting point of a new apologia for sadism."

My father never tired of glorifying this extraordinary element—matter.

"There is no dead matter," he taught us, "lifelessness

is only a disguise behind which hide unknown forms of life. The range of these forms is infinite and their shades and nuances limitless. The Demiurge was in possession of important and interesting creative recipes. Thanks to them, he created a multiplicity of species which renew themselves by their own devices. No one knows whether these recipes will ever be reconstructed. But this is unnecessary, because even if the classical methods of creation should prove inaccessible for evermore, there still remain some illegal methods, an infinity of heretical and criminal methods."

As my father proceeded from these general principles of cosmogony to the more restricted sphere of his private interests, his voice sank to an impressive whisper, the lecture became more and more complicated and difficult to follow, and the conclusions which he reached became more dubious and dangerous. His gestures acquired an esoteric solemnity. He half-closed one eye, put two fingers to his forehead while a look of extraordinary slyness came over his face. He transfixed his listeners with these looks, violated with his cynical expression their most intimate and most private reserve, until he had reached them in the furthest corner whither they had retreated, pressed them against the wall, and tickled them with the finger of irony, finally producing a glimmer of understanding laughter, the laughter of agreement and admission, the visible sign of capitulation.

The girls sat perfectly still, the lamp smoked, the piece of material under the needle of the sewing machine had long since slipped to the floor, and the machine ran empty, stitching only the black, starless cloth unwinding from the bale of winter darkness outside the window.

"We have lived for too long under the terror of the

matchless perfection of the Demiurge," my father said. "For too long the perfection of his creation has paralyzed our own creative instinct. We don't wish to compete with him. We have no ambition to emulate him. We wish to be creators in our own, lower sphere; we want to have the privilege of creation, we want creative delights, we want—in one word—Demiurgy." I don't know on whose behalf my father was proclaiming these demands, what community or corporation, sect or order supported him loyally and lent the necessary weight to his words. As for us, we did not share these demiurgical aspirations.

But Father had meanwhile developed the program of this second Demiurgy, the picture of the second Genesis of creatures which was to stand in open opposition to the present era.

"We are not concerned," he said, "with long-winded creations, with long-term beings. Our creatures will not be heroes of romances in many volumes. Their roles will be short, concise; their characters—without a background. Sometimes, for one gesture, for one word alone, we shall make the effort to bring them to life. We openly admit: we shall not insist either on durability or solidity of workmanship; our creations will be temporary, to serve for a single occasion. If they be human beings, we shall give them, for example, only one profile, one hand, one leg, the one limb needed for their role. It would be pedantic to bother about the other, unnecessary, leg. Their backs can be made of canvas or simply whitewashed. We shall have this proud slogan as our aim: A different actor for every gesture. For each action, each word, we shall call to life a different human being. Such is our whim, and the world will be run according to our pleasure. The Demiurge was in love with consummate, superb, and complicated materials; we shall give priority to trash. We are simply entranced and enchanted by the cheapness, shabbiness, and inferiority of material.

"Can you understand," asked my father, "the deep meaning of that weakness, that passion for colored tissue, for papier-mâché, for distemper, for oakum and sawdust? This is," he continued with a pained smile, "the proof of our love for matter as such, for its fluffiness or porosity, for its unique mystical consistency. Demiurge, that great master and artist, made matter invisible, made it disappear under the surface of life. We, on the contrary, love its creaking, its resistance, its clumsiness. We like to see behind each gesture, behind each move, its inertia, its heavy effort, its bearlike awkwardness."

The girls sat motionless, with glazed eyes. Their faces were long and stultified by listening, their cheeks flushed, and it would have been difficult to decide at that moment whether they belonged to the first or the second Genesis of Creation.

humor

"In one word," Father concluded, "we wish to create man a second time—in the shape and semblance of a tailor's dummy."

Here, for reasons of accuracy, we must describe an insignificant small incident which occurred at that point of the lecture and to which we do not attach much importance. The incident, completely nonsensical and incomprehensible in the sequence of events, could probably be explained as vestigial automatism, without cause and effect, as an instance of the malice of inanimate objects transferred into the region of psychology. We advise the reader to treat it as lightly as we are doing. Here is what happened:

Just as my father pronounced the word "dummy," Adela looked at her wristwatch and exchanged a knowing look with Polda. She then moved her chair forward and, without getting up from it, lifted her dress to reveal her foot tightly covered in black silk, and then stretched it out stiffly like a serpent's head.

She sat thus throughout that scene, upright, her large eyes, shining from atropine, fluttering, while Polda and Pauline sat at her sides. All three looked at Father with wide-open eyes. My father coughed nervously, fell silent, and suddenly became very red in the face. Within a minute the lines of his face, so expressive and vibrant a moment before, became still and his expression became humble.

He—the inspired Heresiarch, just emerging from the clouds of exaltation—suddenly collapsed and folded up. Or perhaps he had been exchanged for another man? That other man now sat stiffly, very flushed, with downcast eyes. Polda went up to him and bent over him. Patting him lightly on the back, she spoke in the tone of gentle encouragement: "Jacob must be sensible. Jacob must obey. Jacob must not be obstinate. Please, Jacob . . . Please. . . ."

Adela's outstretched slipper trembled slightly and shone like a serpent's tongue. My father rose slowly, still looking down, took a step forward like an automaton, and fell to his knees. The lamp hissed in the silence of the room, eloquent looks ran up and down in the thicket of wallpaper patterns, whispers of venomous tongues floated in the air, zigzags of thought. . . .

Treatise on Tailors' Dummies: Continuation

The next evening Father reverted with renewed enthusiasm to his dark and complex subject. Each wrinkle of his deeply lined face expressed incredible cunning. In each fold of skin, a missile of irony lay hidden. But occasionally inspiration widened the spirals of his wrinkles and they swelled horribly and sank in silent whorls into the depths of the winter night.

"Figures in a waxwork museum," he began, "even fair-ground parodies of dummies, must not be treated lightly. Matter never makes jokes: it is always full of the tragically serious. Who dares to think that you can play with matter, that you can shape it for a joke, that the joke will not be built in, will not eat into it like fate, like destiny? Can you imagine the pain, the dull imprisoned suffering, hewn into the matter of that dummy which does not know why it must be what it is, why it must remain in that forcibly imposed form which is no more than a parody? Do you understand the power of form, of expression, of pretense, the arbitrary tyranny imposed on a helpless block, and ruling it like its own, tyrannical, despotic soul? You give a head of canvas and oakum an expression of anger and leave it with it, with the convulsion, the tension enclosed once and for all, with a blind fury for which there is no outlet. The crowd laughs at the parody. Weep, ladies, over your own fate, when you see the misery of imprisoned matter, of tortured matter which does not know what it is and why it is, nor where the gesture may lead that has been imposed on it for ever.

"The crowd laughs. Do you understand the terrible sadism, the exhilarating, demiurgical cruelty of that laughter? Yet we should weep, ladies, at our own fate, when we see that misery of violated matter, against which a terrible wrong has been committed. Hence the frightening sadness of all those jesting golems, of all effigies which brood tragically over their comic grimaces.

"Look at the anarchist Luccheni, the murderer of the
Empress Elizabeth of Austria; look at Draga, the diaboli-
cal and unhappy Queen of Serbia; look at that youth of
genius, the hope and pride of his ancient family, ruined
by the unfortunate habit of masturbation. Oh, the irony
of those names, of those pretensions!

"Is there anything left of Queen Draga in the wax-
figure likeness, any similarity, even the most remote
shadow of her being? But the resemblance, the pretense,
the name reassures us and stops us from asking what that
unfortunate figure is in itself and by itself. And yet it must
be somebody, somebody anonymous, menacing, and unhappy, some being that in its dumb existence had never
heard of Queen Draga. . . .

"Have you heard at night the terrible howling of these
wax figures, shut in the fair-booths; the pitiful chorus of
those forms of wood or porcelain, banging their fists
against the walls of their prisons?"

In my father's face, convulsed by the horror of the
visions which he had conjured up from darkness, a spiral
of wrinkles appeared, a maelstrom growing deeper and
deeper, at the bottom of which there flared the terrible
eye of a prophet. His beard bristled grotesquely, the tufts
of hair growing from warts and moles and from his nostrils stood on end. He became rigid and stood with flaming eyes, trembling from an internal conflict like an automaton of which the mechanism has broken down.

Adela rose from her chair and asked us to avert our
eyes from what was to follow. Then she went up to Father
and, with her hands on her hips in a pose of great deter-
mination, she spoke very clearly.

The two other girls sat stiffly, with downcast eyes,
strangely numb. . . .

Treatise on Tailors' Dummies: Conclusion

On one of the following evenings, my father continued his lecture thus: "When I announced my talk about lay figures, I had not really wanted to speak about those incarnate misunderstandings, those sad parodies that are the fruits of a common and vulgar lack of restraint. I had something else in mind."

Here my father began to set before our eyes the picture of that *generatio aequivoca* which he had dreamed up, a species of beings only half organic, a kind of pseudofauna and pseudoflora, the result of a fantastic fermentation of matter.

They were creations resembling, in appearance only, living creatures such as crustaceans, vertebrates, cephalopods. In reality the appearance was misleading—they were amorphous creatures, with no internal structure, products of the imitative tendency of matter which, equipped with memory, repeats from force of habit the forms already accepted. The morphological scope of matter is limited on the whole and a certain quota of forms is repeated over and over again on various levels of existence.

These creatures—mobile, sensitive to stimuli, and yet outside the pale of real life—could be brought forth by suspending certain complex colloids in solutions of kitchen salt. These colloids, after a number of days, would form and organize themselves in precipitations of substance resembling lower forms of fauna.

In creatures conceived in this way, one could observe the processes of respiration and metabolism, but chemical analysis revealed in them traces neither of albumen nor of carbon compounds.

Yet these primitive forms were unremarkable compared with the richness of shapes and the splendor of the pseudofauna and pseudoflora, which sometimes appeared in certain strictly defined environments, such as old apartments saturated with the emanations of numerous existences and events; used-up atmospheres, rich in the specific ingredients of human dreams; rubbish heaps, abounding in the humus of memories, of nostalgia, and of sterile boredom. On such a soil, this pseudovegetation sprouted abundantly yet ephemerally, brought forth short-lived generations which flourished suddenly and splendidly, only to wilt and perish.

In apartments of that kind, wallpapers must be very weary and bored with the incessant changes in all the cadenzas of rhythm; no wonder that they are susceptible to distant, dangerous dreams. The essence of furniture is unstable, degenerate, and receptive to abnormal temptations: it is then that on this sick, tired, and wasted soil colorful and exuberant mildew can flourish in a fantastic growth, like a beautiful rash.

"As you will no doubt know," said my father, "in old apartments there are rooms which are sometimes forgotten. Unvisited for months on end, they wilt neglected between the old walls and it happens that they close in on themselves, become overgrown with bricks, and, lost once and for all to our memory, forfeit their only claim to existence. The doors, leading to them from some backstairs landing, have been overlooked by people living in the apartment for so long that they merge with the wall, grow into it, and all trace of them is obliterated in a complicated design of lines and cracks.

"Once early in the morning toward the end of winter," my father continued, "after many months of absence, I entered such a forgotten passage, and I was amazed at the appearance of the rooms.

"From all the crevices in the floor, from all the moldings, from every recess, there grew slim shoots filling the gray air with a scintillating filigree lace of leaves: a hothouse jungle, full of whispers and flicking lights—a false and blissful spring. Around the bed, under the lamp, along the wardrobes, grew clumps of delicate trees which, high above, spread their luminous crowns and fountains of lacy leaves, spraying chlorophyll, and thrusting up to the painted heaven of the ceiling. In the rapid process of blossoming, enormous white and pink flowers opened among the leaves, bursting from bud under your very eyes, displaying their pink pulp and spilling over to shed their petals and fall apart in quick decay.

"I was happy," said my father, "to see that unexpected flowering which filled the air with a soft rustle, a gentle murmur, falling like colored confetti through the thin rods of the twigs.

"I could see the trembling of the air, the fermentation of too rich an atmosphere which provoked that precocious blossoming, luxuriation, and wilting of the fantastic oleanders which had filled the room with a rare, lazy snowstorm of large pink clusters of flowers.

"Before nightfall," concluded my father, "there was no trace left of that splendid flowering. The whole elusive sight was a fata morgana, an example of the strange make-believe of matter which had created a semblance of life."

My father was strangely animated that day; the expression in his eyes—a sly, ironic expression—was vivid and humorous. Later he suddenly became more serious and again analyzed the infinite diversity of forms which the multifarious matter could adopt. He was fascinated by doubtful and problematic forms, like the ectoplasm of a medium, by pseudomatter, the cataleptic emanations of the brain which in some instances spread from the mouth of the person in a trance over the whole table, filled the whole room, a floating, rarefied tissue, an astral dough, on the borderline between body and soul.

"Who knows," he said, "how many suffering, crippled, fragmentary forms of life there are, such as the artificially created life of chests and tables quickly nailed together, crucified timbers, silent martyrs to cruel human inventiveness. The terrible transplantation of incompatible and hostile races of wood, their merging into one misbegotten personality.

"How much ancient suffering is there in the varnished grain, in the veins and knots of our old familiar wardrobes? Who would recognize in them the old features, smiles, and glances, almost planed and polished out of all recognition?"

father's fear of being forgotten

My father's face, when he said that, dissolved into a thoughtful net of wrinkles, began to resemble an old plank full of knots and veins, from which all memories had been planed away. For a moment we thought that Father would fall into a state of apathy, which sometimes took hold of him, but all of a sudden he recovered himself and continued to speak:

"Ancient, mythical tribes used to embalm their dead. The walls of their houses were filled with bodies and heads immured in them: a father would stand in a corner of the living room—stuffed, the tanned skin of a deceased wife would serve as a mat under the table. I knew a certain sea captain who had in his cabin a lamp, made by Malayan embalmers from the body of his murdered mistress. On her head, she wore enormous antlers. In the stillness of the cabin, the face stretched between the antlers at the ceiling, slowly lifted its eyelids: on the half-opened lips a bubble of saliva would glint, then burst with the softest of whispers. Octopuses, tortoises, and enormous crabs, hanging from the rafters in place of chandeliers, moved their legs endlessly in that stillness, walking, walking, walking without moving. . . ."

My father's face suddenly assumed a worried, sad expression when his thoughts, stirred by who knows what associations, prompted him to new examples:

"Am I to conceal from you," he said in a low tone, "that my own brother, as a result of a long and incurable illness, has been gradually transformed into a bundle of rubber tubing, and that my poor cousin had to carry him day and night on his cushion, singing to the luckless creature endless lullabies on winter nights? Can there be anything sadder than a human being changed into the rubber tube of an enema? What disappointment for his parents, what confusion for their feelings, what frustration of the hopes centered around the promising youth! And yet, the faithful love of my poor cousin was not denied him even during that transformation."

"Oh, please, I cannot, I really cannot listen to this any longer!" groaned Polda leaning over her chair. "Make him stop, Adela. . . ."

The girls got up, Adela went up to my father with an outstretched finger made as if to tickle him. Father lost countenance, immediately stopped talking, and, very frightened, began to back away from Adela's moving finger. She followed him, however, threatening him with her finger, driving him, step by step, out of the room. Pauline yawned and stretched herself. She and Polda, leaning against one another, exchanged a look and a smile.

Nimrod

I spent the whole of August of that year playing with a splendid little dog that appeared one day on the kitchen floor, awkward and squeaking, still smelling of milk and infancy, with a round, still unformed, and trembling head, paws like a mole's, spreading to the sides, and the most delicate, silky-soft coat.

From the moment I first saw it, that crumb of life won the whole enthusiasm and admiration of which I was capable.

From what heavens had that favorite of the gods descended, to become closer to my heart than all the most beautiful toys? To think that an old, completely uninteresting charwoman could have had the wonderful idea to bring from her home in the suburbs—at a very early, transcendental hour—such a lovely dog to our kitchen!

Ah! one had still been absent—alas—not yet brought back from the dark bosom of sleep, when that happiness had been fulfilled and was waiting for us, lying awkwardly on the cool floor of the kitchen, unappreciated by Adela and the other members of the household. Why had I not been wakened earlier? The saucer of milk on the floor bore witness to Adela's maternal instincts, bore witness, too, unfortunately, to moments lost to me forever from the joys of parenthood.

But before me, all the future lay open. What a prospect of new experiences, experiments, and discoveries! The most essential secret of life, reduced to this simple, handy, toylike form was revealed here to my insatiable curiosity. It was overwhelmingly interesting to have as one's own that scrap of life, that particle of the eternal mystery in a new and amusing shape, which by its very strangeness, by the unexpected transposition of the spark of life, present in us human beings, into a different, animal form, awoke in me an infinite curiosity.

Animals! the object of insatiable interest, examples of the riddle of life, created, as it were, to reveal the human being to man himself, displaying his richness and complexity in a thousand kaleidoscopic possibilities, each of them brought to some curious end, to some characteristic exuberance. Still unburdened by the complications of eccentric interests which spoil relationships between people, my heart was filled with sympathy for that manifestation of the eternity of life, with a loving tender curiosity that was identical with self-revelation.

The dog was warm and as soft as velvet and had a small quick heartbeat. He had two petal-soft ears, opaque blue eyes, a pink mouth into which one could put one's finger with impunity, delicate and innocent paws with enchanting pink warts on the outside, over the fore-toes. He crept with these paws right into a bowl of milk, greedy and impatient, lapping it up with his pale red tongue.

When he had had enough he would sadly lift his small muzzle, with drops of milk hanging from it, and retreat clumsily from the milky bath.

He walked with an awkward oblique roll in an undecided direction, along a shaky and uncertain line. His usual mood was one of indefinite basic sadness. He had the dejected helplessness of an orphan—an inability to fill the emptiness of life between the sensational events of meals. This was reflected in the aimlessness of his movements, in his irrational fits of melancholia, his sad whimpering, and his inability to settle down in any one place. Even in the depths of sleep, in which he had to satisfy his need for protection and love by curling himself up into a trembling ball, he could not rid himself of the feeling of loneliness and homelessness. Oh, how a young and meager life, brought forth from familiar darkness, from the homely warmth of a mother's womb into a large, foreign, bright world, shrinks and retreats and recoils from accepting the undertaking—and with what aversion and disappointment!

But slowly, little Nimrod (for that was the proud and martial name we gave him) began to like life better. His exclusive preoccupation with longing for a return to the maternal womb gave way before the charms of plurality.

The world began to set traps for him: the unknown and tantalizing taste of various foods, the square patch of morning sunlight on the floor in which it was so pleasant to rest, the movements of his own limbs, his own paws, his tail roguishly inviting him to play, the fondling of human hands which induced a certain playfulness, the gaiety that filled him with a need for completely new, violent, and risky movements—all this tricked and encouraged him to the acceptance of the experiment of life and to submission to it.

One more thing: Nimrod began to understand that what he was experiencing was, in spite of its appearance of novelty, something which had existed before—many times before. His body began to recognize situations, impressions, and objects. In reality, none of these astonished him very much. Faced with new circumstances, he would dip into the fount of his memory, the deep-seated memory of the body, would search blindly and feverishly, and often find ready-made within himself a suitable reaction: the wisdom of generations, deposited in his plasma, in his nerves. He found actions and decisions of which he had not been aware but which had been lying in wait, ready to emerge.

The backdrop of his young life, the kitchen with its buckets and cloths full of complicated and intriguing smells, the clacking of Adela's slippers and her noisy bustle, ceased to frighten him. He got used to considering it his domain, began to feel at home in it and to develop vague feeling of belonging to it, almost of patriotism.

Unless of course there was a sudden cataclysm in the shape of floor scrubbing—an abolition of the laws of nature—the splashing of warm lye, flooding all the furniture and the loud scraping of Adela's brushes.

But the danger passed; the brush, now calm and immobile, returned to its corner, the floor smelled sweetly of damp wood. Nimrod, restored again to his normal rights and to the freedom of his own territory, would have a sudden urge to grab an old rug between his teeth and to tear at it with all his strength, pulling it to the left and to the right. The pacification of the elements filled him with indescribable joy.

Suddenly he stopped still: in front of him, some three puppy steps away, there appeared a black monster, a scarecrow moving quickly on the rods of many entangled legs. Deeply shaken, Nimrod's eyes followed the course of the shiny insect, observing tensely the flat, apparently headless torso, carried with uncanny speed by the spidery legs.

Something stirred in him at that sight, a feeling which he could not yet understand, a mixture of anger and fear, rather pleasurable and combined with a shiver of strength, of self-assertion, of aggression.

And suddenly he dropped onto his forepaws and uttered a sound unfamiliar to him, a strange noise, completely different from his usual whimpering. He uttered it once, then again and again, in a thin faltering descant.

But in vain did he apostrophize the insect in this new language, born of sudden inspiration, as a cockroach's understanding is not equal to such a tirade: the insect continued on its journey to a corner of the room, with movements sanctified by an ageless ritual of the cockroach world.

The feeling of loathing had as yet no permanence or strength in the dog's soul. The newly awakened joy of life transformed every sensation into a great joke, into gaiety. Nimrod kept on barking, but the tone of it had changed imperceptibly, had become a parody of what it had been—an attempt to express the incredible wonder of that capital enterprise, life, so full of unexpected encounters, pleasures, and thrills.

Pan

   In a corner between the backs of sheds and out-
buildings was a blind alley leading from the courtyard;
the farthest, ultimate cul-de-sac, hemmed in between the
privy and the wall of the chicken run—a dismal spot,
beyond which one could see no farther.

   This was the land's end, the Gibraltar of the courtyard,
desperately knocking its head against the blind fence of
horizontal planks, enclosing that little world with finality.

   From under the fence ran a rivulet of black, stinking
water, a vein of rotting greasy mud which never dried
out—the only road which led across the border of the
fence into the wider world. The despair of the fetid
alleyway had pushed for so long against the obstacle of
the fence that it had loosened one of its planks. We boys
did the rest and prised the plank free. In this way we
made a breach, opening a window to the sun. Putting a
foot on the plank which we had thrown as a bridge across
the puddle, the prisoner of the courtyard could squeeze
through the crack and let himself out into a new, wider

world of fresh breezes. There, spread out before him, was a large, overgrown garden. Tall pear trees, broad apple trees, grew there in profusion, covered with silvery rustling leaves, with a foaming white glinting net. Thick tangled grass, never cut, covered the undulating ground with a fluffy carpet. Common meadow grasses with feathery heads grew there; wild parsley with its delicate filigrees; ground ivy with rough wrinkled leaves, and dead nettles smelling of mint. Shiny sinewy plantains spotted with rust shot up to display bunches of thick red seeds. The whole of this jungle was soaked in the gentle air and filled with blue breezes. When you lay in the grass you were under the azure map of clouds and sailing continents, you inhaled the whole geography of the sky. From that communion with the air, the leaves and blades became covered with delicate hair, with a soft layer of down, a rough bristle of hooks made, it seemed, to grasp and hold the waves of oxygen. That delicate and whitish layer related the vegetation to the atmosphere, gave it the silvery grayish tint of the air, of shadowy silences between two glimpses of the sun. And one of the plants, yellow, inflated with air, its pale stems full of milky juice, brought forth from its empty shoots only pure air, pure down in the shape of fluffy dandelion balls scattered by the wind to dissolve noiselessly into the blue silence.

The garden was vast with a number of extensions, and had various zones and climates. From one side it was open to the sky and air, and there it offered the softest, most delicate bed of fluffy green. But where the ground extended into a low-lying isthmus and dropped into the shadow of the back wall of a deserted soda factory, it became grimmer, overgrown and wild with neglect, untidy, fierce with thistles, bristling with nettles, covered with a rash of weeds, until, at the very end between the walls, in an open rectangular bay, it lost all moderation and became insane. There, it was an orchard no more, but a paroxysm of madness, an outbreak of fury, of cynical shamelessness and lust. There, bestially liberated, giving full rein to their passion, ruled the empty, overgrown, cabbage heads of burs—enormous witches, shedding their voluminous skirts in broad daylight, throwing them down, one by one, until their swollen, rustling, hole-riddled rags buried the whole quarrelsome bastard breed under their crazy expanse. And still the skirts swelled and pushed, piling up one on top of another, spreading and growing all the time—a mass of tinny leaves reaching up to the low eaves of a shed.

It was there that I saw him first and for the only time in my life, at a noon-hour crazy with heat. It was at a moment when time, demented and wild, breaks away from the treadmill of events and like an escaping vagabond, runs shouting across the fields. Then the summer grows out of control, spreads at all points all over space with a wild impetus, doubling and trebling itself into an unknown, lunatic dimension.

At that hour, I submitted to the frenzy of chasing butterflies, to the passion of pursuing these shimmering spots, these errant white flakes, trembling in awkward zigzags in the burning air. And it so happened that one of these spots of light divided during flight into two, then into three—and the shining, blindingly white triangle of spots led me, like a will-o'-the-wisp, through the jungle of thistles, scorched by the sun.

I stopped at the edge of the burs, not daring to advance into that hollow abyss.

And then, suddenly, I saw him.

Submerged up to his armpits in the thicket of burs, he crouched in front of me.

I saw his broad back in a dirty shirt and the grubby side of his jacket. He sat there, as if ready to leap, his shoulders hunched as under a great burden. His body panted with tension, and perspiration streamed down his copper-brown face, glinting in the sun. Immobile, he seemed to be working very hard, struggling under some enormous weight.

I stood, nailed to the spot by his look, held captive by it.

It was the face of a tramp or a drunkard. A tuft of filthy hair bristled over his broad forehead, rounded like a stone washed by a stream. That forehead was now creased into deep furrows. I did not know whether it was the pain, the burning heat of the sun, or that superhuman effort that had eaten into his face and stretched those features near to cracking. His dark eyes bored into me with the fixedness of supreme despair or of suffering. He both looked at me and did not, he saw me and did not see. His eyes were like bursting shells, strained in a transport of pain or the wild delights of inspiration.

And suddenly on those taut features there slowly spread a terrible grimace. The grimace intensified, taking in the previous madness and tension, swelling, becoming broader and broader, until it broke into a roaring, hoarse shout of laughter.

Deeply shaken, I saw how, still roaring with laughter, he slowly lifted himself up from his crouching position and, hunched like a gorilla, his hands in the torn pockets of his ragged trousers, began to run, cutting in great leaps and bounds through the rustling tinfoil of the burs —a Pan without a pipe, retreating in flight to his familiar haunts.

Mr. Charles

Early on Saturday afternoon my Uncle Charles, a grass widower, set out for a holiday resort, an hour's walk from the city, to visit his wife and children, who were spending the summer there.

Since his wife's departure, the house had not been cleaned, the bed not made. Charles returned home late at night, battered and bruised by the nightly revels to which he succumbed under the pressure of the hot empty days. The crushed, cool, disordered bedclothes seemed like a blissful haven, an island of safety on which he succeeded in landing with the last ounce of his strength like a castaway, tossed for many days and nights on a stormy sea.

Groping blindly in the darkness, he sank between the white mounds of cool feathers and slept as he fell, across the bed or with his head downward, pushing deep into the softness of the pillows, as if in sleep he wanted to drill through, to explore completely, that powerful massif of feather-bedding rising out of the night. He fought in his sleep against the bed like a bather swimming against the current, he kneaded it and molded it with his body like an enormous bowl of dough, and woke up at dawn panting, covered with sweat, thrown up on the shores of that pile of bedding which he could not master in the nightly struggle. Half-landed from the depth of unconsciousness, he still hung on to the verge of night, gasping for breath, while the bedding grew around him, swelled and fermented—and again engulfed him in a mountain of heavy, whitish dough.

He slept thus until late morning, while the pillows arranged themselves into a large flat plain on which his now quieter sleep would wander. On these white roads, he slowly returned to his senses, to daylight, to reality— and at last he opened his eyes as does a sleeping passenger when the train stops at a station.

Stale dusk filled the room with the dregs of many days of solitude and quietness. The window buzzed with the morning swarms of flies and only the curtains shone brightly. Charles yawned out of his body, out of the depth of all its cavities the remains of yesterday. The yawning was convulsive as if his body wanted to turn itself inside out. In this way he got rid of the sand and ballast, the undigested remains of the previous day.

Having thus eased himself, he wrote down his expenses in a notebook, calculated something, added it all up, and became pensive. Then he lay immobile for a long time, with glazed eyes which were the color of water, protuberant and moist. In the diffused dusk of the room, brightened by the glare of the hot day behind the curtains, his eyes, like minuscule mirrors, reflected all the shining objects: the white light of the sun in the cracks of the window, the golden rectangle of the curtains, and enclosed, like a drop of water, all the room with the stillness of its carpets and its empty chairs.

Meanwhile, the day behind the blinds resounded more and more violently with the buzzing of flies frenzied by the sun. The window could not contain this white fire and the curtains went faint from the bright undulations.

At last Charles dragged himself from the bed and sat on it for some time, groaning. Past thirty, his body was beginning to thicken. His system, swelling with fat, harassed by sexual indulgence, but still flowing with seminal juices, seemed slowly to shape, in that silence, its future destiny.

While Charles sat there in a thoughtless, vegetative stupor, completely surrendered to circulation, respiration, and the deep pulsation of his natural juices, there formed inside his perspiring body an unknown, unformulated future, like a terrible growth, pushing forth in an unknown direction. He was not afraid of it, because he already felt at one with that unknown and enormous thing which was to come, and he was growing together with it without protest, in a strange unison, numb with resigned awe, recognizing his future self in those colossal exuberances, those fantastic tumors which were maturing before his inward-turned sight. One of his eyes would then slightly squint to the outside, as if leaving for another dimension.

Afterward, he awoke from those hopeless musings, returning to the reality of the moment. He looked at his feet on the carpet, plump and delicate like a woman's, and slowly removed his gold cuff links from the cuffs of his shirt. Then he went to the kitchen and in a shady corner found a bucket of water, a round, silent, watchful mirror waiting for him—the only living and knowing thing in that empty flat. He poured water into the basin and tasted with his skin its young, sweet, stale moisture.

He dressed with care, but without haste, with long pauses between the separate manipulations.

The rooms, empty and neglected, did not approve of him, the furniture and the walls watched him in silent criticism.

He felt, entering that stillness, like an intruder in an underwater kingdom with a different, separate notion of time.

Opening his own drawers, he felt like a thief and could not help moving on tiptoe, afraid to arouse noisy and excessive echoes that waited irritably for the chance to explode on the slightest provocation.

And finally, when after sneaking from dresser to closet, he had found piece by piece all he needed and had finished his dressing among the furniture which bore with him in silence, and was ready at last, he stood, hat in hand, feeling rather embarrassed that even at the last moment he could not find a word which would dispel that hostile silence; he then walked toward the door slowly, resignedly, hanging his head, while someone else, someone forever turning his back, walked at the same pace in the opposite direction into the depths of the mirror, through the row of empty rooms which did not exist.

Cinnamon Shops

At the time of the shortest, sleepy winter days, edged on both sides with the furry dusk of mornings and evenings, when the city reached out deeper and deeper into the labyrinth of winter nights, and was shaken reluctantly into consciousness by the short dawn, my father was already lost, sold and surrendered to the other sphere.

His face and head became overgrown with a wild and recalcitrant shock of gray hair, bristling in irregular tufts and spikes, shooting out from warts, from his eyebrows, from the openings of his nostrils and giving him the appearance of an old ill-tempered fox.

His sense of smell and his hearing sharpened extraordinarily and one could see from the expression of his tense silent face that through the intermediary of these two senses he remained in permanent contact with the unseen world of mouseholes, dark corners, chimney vents, and dusty spaces under the floor.

He was a vigilant and attentive observer, a prying fellow conspirator, of the rustlings, the nightly creakings, the secret gnawing life of the floor. He was so engrossed in it that he became completely submerged in an inaccessible sphere and one which he did not even attempt to discuss with us.

(He often used to flip his fingers and laugh softly to himself when the manifestations of the unseen became too absurd) he then exchanged knowing looks with our cat, which, also initiated in these mysteries, would lift its cynical cold striped face, closing the slanting chinks of its eyes with an air of indifference and boredom.

It sometimes happened that, during a meal, my father would suddenly put aside his knife and fork and, with his napkin still tied around his neck, would rise from the table with a feline movement, tiptoe to the door of the adjoining room and peer through the keyhole with the utmost caution. Then, with a bashful smile, he would return to the table slightly embarrassed, murmuring and whispering indistinctly in tune with the interior monologue that wholly preoccupied him.

(To provide some distraction for him and to tear him away from these morbid speculations, my mother would force him to go out for a walk in the evenings.) He went in silence, without protest but also without enthusiasm, distrait and absent in spirit. Once we even went all together to the theater.

We found ourselves again in that large, badly lit, dirty hall, full of somnolent human chatter and aimless confusion. But when we had made our way through the crowd, there emerged before us an enormous pale-blue curtain, like the sky of another firmament. Large, painted pink masks, with puffed-up cheeks floated in a huge expanse of canvas. The artificial sky spread out in both directions, swelling with the powerful breath of pathos and of great gestures, with the atmosphere of that fictitious floodlit world created on the echoing scaffoldings of the stage. The tremor sailing across the large area of that sky, the breath of the vast canvas which made the masks revive and grow, revealed the illusory character of that firmament, caused that vibration of reality which, in metaphysical moments, we experience as the glimmer of revelation.

The masks fluttered their red eyelids, their colored lips whispered voicelessly, and I knew that the moment was imminent when the tension of mystery would reach its zenith and the swollen skies of the curtain would really burst open to reveal incredible and dazzling events.

But I was not allowed to experience that moment, because in the meantime my father had begun to betray a certain anxiety. He was feeling in all his pockets and at last declared that he had left behind at home a wallet containing money and certain most important documents.

After a short conference with my mother, during which Adela's honesty was submitted to a hasty assessment, it was suggested that I should go home to look for the wallet. According to my mother, there was still plenty of time before the curtain rose and, fleet-footed as I was, I had every chance of returning in time.

(I stepped into a winter night bright from the illuminations of the sky) It was one of those clear nights when the starry firmament is so wide and spreads so far that it seems to be divided and broken up into a mass of separate skies, sufficient for a whole month of winter nights and providing silver and painted globes to cover all the nightly phenomena, adventures, occurrences, and carnivals.

It is exceedingly thoughtless to send a young boy out on an urgent and important errand into a night like that, because in its semiobscurity the streets multiply, becoming confused and interchanged. There open up, deep inside a city, reflected streets, streets which are doubles, make-believe streets. One's imagination, bewitched and misled, creates illusory maps of the apparently familiar districts, maps in which the streets have their proper places and usual names but are provided with new and fictitious configurations by the inexhaustible inventiveness of the night. The temptations of such winter nights begin usually with the innocent desire to take a shortcut, to use a quicker but less familiar way. Attractive possibilities arise of shortening a complicated walk by taking some never used side street. But on that occasion things began differently.

Having taken a few steps, I realized that I was not wearing my overcoat. I wanted to turn back, but after a moment that seemed to me an unnecessary waste of time, especially as the night was not cold at all; on the contrary, I could feel waves of an unseasonal warmth, like breezes of a spring night. The snow shrank into a white fluff, into a harmless fleece smelling sweetly of violets. Similar white fluffs were sailing across the sky on which the moon was doubled and trebled, showing all its phases and positions at once.

On that night the sky laid bare its internal construction in many sections which, like quasi-anatomical exhibits, showed the spirals and whorls of light, the pale-green solids of darkness, the plasma of space, the tissue of dreams.

On such a night, it was impossible to walk along Rampart Street, or any other of the dark streets which are the obverse, the lining as it were, of the four sides of Market Square, and not to remember that at that late hour the strange and most attractive shops were sometimes open, the shops which on ordinary days one tended to overlook. I used to call them cinnamon shops because of the dark paneling of their walls.

These truly noble shops, open late at night, have always been the objects of my ardent interest. Dimly lit, their dark and solemn interiors were redolent of the smell of paint, varnish, and incense; of the aroma of distant countries and rare commodities. You could find in them Bengal lights, magic boxes, the stamps of long-forgotten countries, Chinese decals, indigo, calaphony from Malabar, the eggs of exotic insects, parrots, toucans, live salamanders and basilisks, mandrake roots, mechanical toys from Nuremberg, homunculi in jars, microscopes, binoculars, and, most especially, strange and rare books, old folio volumes full of astonishing engravings and amazing stories.

I remember those old dignified merchants who served their customers with downcast eyes, in discreet silence, and who were full of wisdom and tolerance for their customers' most secret whims. But most of all, I remember a bookshop in which I once glanced at some rare and forbidden pamphlets, the publications of secret societies lifting the veil on tantalizing and unknown mysteries.

I so rarely had the occasion to visit these shops—especially with a small but sufficient amount of money in my pocket—that I could not forgo the opportunity I had now, in spite of the important mission entrusted to me.

According to my calculations I ought to turn into a

narrow lane and pass two or three side streets in order to reach the street of the night shops. This would take me even farther from home, but by cutting across Saltworks Street, I could make good the delay.

Lent wings by my desire to visit the cinnamon shops, I turned into a street I knew and ran rather than walked, anxious not to lose my way. I passed three or four streets, but still there was no sign of the turning I wanted. What is more, the appearance of the street was different from what I had expected. Nor was there any sign of the shops. I was in a street of houses with no doors and of which the tightly shut windows were blind from reflected moonlight. On the other side of those houses—I thought—must run the street from which they were accessible. I was walking faster now, rather disturbed, beginning to give up the idea of visiting the cinnamon shops. All I wanted now was to get out of there quickly into some part of the city I knew better. I reached the end of the street, unsure where it would lead me. I found myself in a broad, sparsely built-up avenue, very long and straight. I felt on me the breath of a wide-open space. Close to the pavement or in the midst of their gardens, picturesque villas stood there, the private houses of the rich. In the gaps between them were parks and walls of orchards. The whole area looked like Lesznianska Street in its lower and rarely visited part. The moonlight filtered through a thousand feathery clouds, like silver scales on the sky. It was pale and bright as daylight—only the parks and gardens stood black in that silvery landscape.

Looking more closely at one of the buildings, I realized that what I saw was the back of the high school which I had never seen from that side. I was just approaching the gate which, to my surprise, was open; the entrance hall was lit. I walked in and found myself on the red carpet of the passage. I hoped to be able to slip through unobserved and come out through the front gate, thus taking a splendid shortcut.

(I remembered that at that late hour there might be, in Professor Arendt's classroom, one of the voluntary classes which in winter were always held in the late evenings and to which we all flocked, fired by the enthusiasm for art which that excellent teacher had awakened in us.)

A small group of industrious pupils was almost lost in the large dark hall on whose walls the enormous shadows of our heads broke abruptly, thrown by the light of two small candles set in bottles.

To be truthful, we did not draw very much during these classes and the professor was not very exacting. Some boys brought cushions from home and stretched themselves out on benches for a short nap. Only the most diligent of us gathered around the candle, in the golden circle of its light.

We usually had to wait a long while for the professor's arrival, filling the time with sleepy conversation. At last the door from his room would open and he would enter —short, bearded, given to esoteric smiles and discreet silences and exuding an aroma of secrecy. He shut the door of his study carefully behind him: through it for a brief moment we could see over his head a crowd of plaster shadows, the classical fragments of suffering Niobides, Danaides, and Tantalides, the whole sad and sterile Olympus, wilting for years on end in that plaster-cast museum. The light in his room was opaque even in daytime, thick from the dreams of plaster-cast heads, from empty looks, ashen profiles, and meditations dissolving into nothingness. We liked to listen sometimes in front of that door—listen to the silence laden with the sighs and whispers of the crumbling gods withering in the boredom and monotony of their twilight.

The professor walked with great dignity and unction up and down among the half-empty benches on which, in small groups, we were drawing amidst the gray reflections of a winter night. Everything was quiet and cozy. Some of my classmates were asleep. The candles were burning low in their bottles. The professor delved into a deep bookcase, full of old folios, unfashionable engravings, woodcuts, and prints. He showed us, with his esoteric gestures, old lithographs of night landscapes, of tree clumps in moonlight, of avenues in wintry parks outlined black on the white moonlit background.

Amidst sleepy talk, time passed unnoticed. It ran by unevenly, as if making knots in the passage of hours, swallowing somewhere whole empty periods. Without transition, our whole gang found ourselves on the way home long after midnight on the garden path white with snow, flanked by the black, dry thicket of bushes. We walked alongside that hairy rim of darkness, brushing against the furry bushes, their lower branches snapping under our feet in the bright night, in a false milky brightness. The diffuse whiteness of light filtered by the snow, by the pale air, by the milky space, was like the gray paper of an engraving on which the thick bushes corresponded to the deep black lines of decoration. The night was copying now, at that late hour, the nightly landscapes of Professor Arendt's engravings, re-enacting his fantasies.

In the black thickets of the park, in the hairy coat of bushes, in the mass of crusty twigs there were nooks, niches, nests of deepest fluffy blackness, full of confusion, secret gestures, conniving looks. It was warm and quiet there. We sat on the soft snow in our heavy coats, cracking hazelnuts of which there was a profusion in that springlike winter. Through the copse, weasels wandered silently, martens and ichneumons, furry, ferreting elongated animals on short legs, stinking of sheepskin. We suspected that among them were the exhibits from the school cabinets which, although degutted and molting, felt on that white night in their empty bowels the voice of the eternal instinct, the mating urge, and returned to the thickets for short moments of illusory life.

But slowly the phosphorescence of the springlike snow became dulled: it vanished then, giving way to a thick black darkness preceding dawn. Some of us fell asleep in the warm snow, others went groping in the dark for the doors of their houses and walked blindly into the sleep of their parents and brothers, into a continuation of deep snoring which caught up with them on their late return.

These nightly drawing sessions held a secret charm for me, so that now I could not forgo the opportunity of looking for a moment into the art room. I decided, however, that I would not stop for more than a little while. But walking up the back stairs, their cedar wood resounding under my steps, I realized that I was in a wing of the school building completely unknown to me.

Not even a murmur interrupted the solemn silence. The passages were broader in this wing, covered with a thick carpet and most elegant. Small, darkly glowing lamps were hung at each corner. Turning the first of these, I found myself in an even wider, more sumptuous hall. In one of its walls there was a wide glass arcade leading to the interior of an apartment. I could see a long enfilade of rooms, furnished with great magnificence.

The eye wandered over silk hangings, gilded mirrors, costly furniture, and crystal chandeliers and into the velvety softness of the luxurious interiors, shimmering with lights, entangled garlands, and budding flowers. The profound stillness of these empty rooms was filled with the secret glances exchanged by mirrors and the panic of friezes running high along the walls and disappearing into the stucco of the white ceilings.

I faced all that magnificence with admiration and awe, guessing that my nightly escapade had brought me unexpectedly into the headmaster's wing, to his private apartment. I stood there with a beating heart, rooted to the spot by curiosity, ready to escape at the slightest noise. How would I justify, if surprised, that nocturnal visit, that impudent prying? In one of those deep plush armchairs there might sit, unobserved and still, the young daughter of the headmaster. She might lift her eyes to mine—black, sibylline, quiet eyes, the gaze of which none could hold. But to retreat halfway, not having carried through the plan I had, would be cowardly. Besides, deep silence reigned in those magnificent interiors, lit by the hazy light of an undefined hour. Through the arcades of the passage, I saw on the far side of the living room a large glass door leading to the terrace. It was so still everywhere that I felt suddenly emboldened. It did not strike me as too risky to walk down the short steps leading to the level of the living room, to take a few quick steps across the large, costly carpet and to find myself on the terrace from which I could get back without any difficulty to the familiar street.

This is what I did. When I found myself on the parquet floor under the potted palms that reached up to the frieze of the ceiling, I noticed that now I really was on neutral ground, because the living room did not have a front wall. It was a kind of large loggia, connected by a few steps with a city square, an enclosed part of the square, because some of the garden furniture stood directly on the pavement. I ran down the short flight of stone steps and found myself at street level once more.

The constellations in the sky stood steeply on their heads, all the stars had made an about-turn, but the moon, buried under the featherbed of clouds which were lit by its unseen presence, seemed still to have before her an endless journey and, absorbed in her complicated heavenly procedures, did not think of dawn.

A few horse-drawn cabs loomed black in the street, half-broken and loose-jointed like crippled, dozing crabs or cockroaches. A driver leaned down toward me from his high box. He had a small red, kindly face. "Shall we go, master?" he asked. The cab shook in all the joints and ligatures of its many-limbed body and made a start on its light wheels.

But who would entrust oneself on such a night to the whims of an unpredictable cabby? Amidst the click of the axles, amidst the thud of the box and the roof, I could not agree with him on my destination. He nodded indulgently at everything I said and sang to himself. We drove in a circle around the city.

In front of an inn stood a group of cabbies who waved friendly hands to him. He answered gaily and then, without stopping the carriage, (he threw the reins on my knees, jumped down from the box, and joined the group of his colleagues.) The horse, an old, wise cab horse, looked round cursorily and went on in a monotonous regular trot. In fact, that horse inspired confidence—it seemed smarter than its driver. But I myself could not drive, so I had to rely on the horse's will. We turned into a suburban street, bordered on both sides by gardens. As we advanced, these gardens slowly changed into parks with tall trees and the parks in turn into forests.

I shall never forget that luminous journey on that brightest of winter nights. The colored map of the heavens expanded into an immense dome, on which there loomed fantastic lands, oceans and seas, marked with the lines of stellar currents and eddies, with the brilliant streaks of heavenly geography. The air became light to breathe and shimmered like silver gauze. One could smell violets. From under the white woolly lambskin of snow, trembling anemones appeared with a speck of moonlight in each delicate cup. The whole forest seemed to be illuminated by thousands of lights and by the stars falling in profusion from the December sky. The air pulsated with a secret spring, with the matchless purity of snow and violets. We entered a hilly landscape. The lines of hills, bristling with the bare spikes of trees, rose like sighs of bliss. I saw on these happy slopes groups of wanderers, gathering among the moss and the bushes the fallen stars which now were damp from snow. The road became steep, the horse began to slip on it and pulled the creaking cab only with an effort. I was happy. My lungs soaked up the blissful spring in the air, the freshness of snow and stars. Before the horse's breast the rampart of white snowy foam grew higher and higher, and it could hardly wade through that pure fresh mass. At last we stopped. I got out of the cab. The horse was panting, hanging its head. I hugged its head to my breast and saw that there were tears in its large eyes. I noticed a round black wound on its belly. "Why did not you tell me?" I whispered, crying. "My dearest, I did it for you," the horse said and became very small, like a wooden toy. I left him and felt wonderfully light and happy. I was debating whether to wait for the small local train which passed through here or to walk back to the city. I began to walk down a steep path, winding like a serpent amidst the forest; at first in a light, elastic step; later, passing into a brisk, happy run which became gradually faster, until it resembled a gliding descent on skis. I could regulate my speed at will and change course by light movements of my body.

On the outskirts of the city, I slowed this triumphal run and changed it into a sedate walk. The moon still rode high in the sky. The transformations of the sky, the metamorphoses of its multiple domes into more and more complicated configurations were endless. Like a silver astrolabe the sky disclosed on that magic night its internal mechanism and showed in infinite evolutions the mathematics of its cogs and wheels.

In Market Square I met some people enjoying a walk. All of them, enchanted by the displays of that night, walked with uplifted faces, silvery from the magic of the sky. I completely stopped worrying about Father's wallet. My father, absorbed by his manias, had probably forgotten its loss by now, and as for my mother, I did not much care.

On such a night, unique in the year, one has happy thoughts and inspirations, one feels touched by the divine finger of poetry. Full of ideas and projects, I wanted to walk toward my home, but met some school friends with books under their arms. They were on their way to school already, having been wakened by the brightness of that night that would not end.

We went for a walk all together along a steeply falling street, pervaded by the scent of violets; <u>uncertain whether it was the magic of the night which lay like silver on the snow or whether it was the light of dawn</u>. . . .

The Street of Crocodiles

My father kept in the lower drawer of his large
desk an old and beautiful map of our city. It was a whole
folio sheaf of parchment pages which, originally fastened
with strips of linen, formed an enormous wall map, a
bird's-eye panorama.

Hung on the wall, the map covered it almost entirely
and opened a wide view on the valley of the River Tys-
mienica, which wound itself like a wavy ribbon of pale
gold, on the maze of widely spreading ponds and
marshes, on the high ground rising toward the south,
gently at first, then in ever tighter ranges, in a chessboard
of rounded hills, smaller and paler as they receded toward
the misty yellow fog of the horizon. From that faded
distance of the periphery, the city rose and grew toward
the center of the map, an undifferentiated mass at first, a
dense complex of blocks and houses, cut by deep canyons
of streets, to become on the first plan a group of single
houses, etched with the sharp clarity of a landscape seen

through binoculars. In that section of the map, the engraver concentrated on the complicated and manifold profusion of streets and alleyways, the sharp lines of cornices, architraves, archivolts, and pilasters, lit by the dark gold of a late and cloudy afternoon which steeped all corners and recesses in the deep sepia of shade. The solids and prisms of that shade darkly honeycombed the ravines of streets, drowning in a warm color here half a street, there a gap between houses. They dramatized and orchestrated in a bleak romantic chiaroscuro the complex architectural polyphony.

On that map, made in the style of baroque panoramas, the area of the Street of Crocodiles shone with the empty whiteness that usually marks polar regions or unexplored countries of which almost nothing is known. The lines of only a few streets were marked in black and their names given in simple, unadorned lettering, different from the noble script of the other captions. The cartographer must have been loath to include that district in the city and his reservations found expression in the typographical treatment.

In order to understand these reservations, we must draw attention to the equivocal and doubtful character of that peculiar area, so unlike the rest of the city.

It was an industrial and commercial district, its soberly utilitarian character glaringly underlined. The spirit of the times, the mechanism of economics, had not spared our city and had taken root in a sector of its periphery which then developed into a parasitical quarter.

word choice

While in the old city a nightly semiclandestine trade prevailed, marked by ceremonious solemnity, in the new district modern, sober forms of commercial endeavor had flourished at once. The pseudo-Americanism, grafted on the old, crumbling core of the city, shot up here in a rich but empty and colorless vegetation of pretentious vulgarity. One could see there cheap jerry-built houses with grotesque façades, covered with a monstrous stucco of cracked plaster. The old, shaky suburban houses had large hastily constructed portals grafted on to them which only on close inspection revealed themselves as miserable imitations of metropolitan splendor. Dull, dirty, and faulty glass panes in which dark pictures of the street were wavily reflected, the badly planed wood of the doors, the gray atmosphere of those sterile interiors where the high shelves were cracked and the crumbling walls were covered with cobwebs and thick dust, gave these shops the stigma of some wild Klondike. In row upon row there spread tailors' shops, general outfitters, china stores, drugstores, and barbers' saloons. Their large gray display windows bore slanting semicircular inscriptions in thick gilt letters: CONFISERIE, MANU-CURE, KING OF ENGLAND.

The old established inhabitants of the city kept away from that area where the scum, the lowest orders had settled—creatures without character, without background, moral dregs, that inferior species of human being which is born in such ephemeral communities. But on days of defeat, in hours of moral weakness, it would happen that one or another of the city dwellers would venture half by chance into that dubious district. The best among them were not entirely free from the temptation of voluntary degradation, of breaking down the barriers of hierarchy, of immersion in that shallow mud of companionship, of easy intimacy, of dirty intermingling. The district was an El Dorado for such moral deserters. Everything seemed suspect and equivocal there, everything promised with secret winks, cynically stressed gestures, raised eyebrows, the fulfillment of impure hopes, everything helped to release the lowest instincts from their shackles.

Only a few people noticed the peculiar characteristics of that district: the fatal lack of color, as if that shoddy, quickly-growing area could not afford the luxury of it. Everything was gray there, as in black-and-white photographs or in cheap illustrated catalogues. This similarity was real rather than metaphorical because at times, when wandering in those parts, one in fact gained the impression that one was turning the pages of a prospectus, looking at columns of boring commercial advertisements, among which suspect announcements nestled like parasites, together with dubious notices and illustrations with a double meaning. And one's wandering proved as sterile and pointless as the excitement produced by a close study of pornographic albums.

If one entered for example a tailor's shop to order a suit—a suit of cheap elegance characteristic of the district —one found that the premises were large and empty, the rooms high and colorless. Enormous shelves rose in tiers into the undefined height of the room and drew one's eyes toward the ceiling which might be the sky—the shoddy, faded sky of that quarter. On the other hand, the storerooms, which could be seen through the open door, were stacked high with boxes and crates—an enormous filing cabinet rising to the attic to disintegrate into the geometry of emptiness, into the timbers of a void. The large gray windows, ruled like the pages of a ledger, did not admit daylight yet the shop was filled with a watery anonymous gray light which did not throw shadows and did not stress anything. Soon, a slender young man appeared, astonishingly servile, agile, and compliant, to satisfy one's requirements and to drown one in the smooth flow of his cheap sales talk. But when, talking all the time, he unrolled an enormous piece of cloth, fitting, folding, and draping the stream of material, forming it into imaginary jackets and trousers, that whole manipulation seemed suddenly unreal, a sham comedy, a screen ironically placed to hide the true meaning of things.

The tall dark salesgirls, each with a flaw in her beauty (appropriately for that district of remaindered goods), came and went, stood in the doorways watching to see whether the business entrusted to the experienced care of the salesman had reached a suitable point. The salesman simpered and pranced around like a transvestite. One wanted to lift up his receding chin or pinch his pale powdered cheek as with a stealthy meaningful look he discreetly pointed to the trademark on the material, a trademark of transparent symbolism.

Slowly the selection of the suit gave place to the second stage of the plan. The effeminate and corrupted youth, receptive to the client's most intimate stirrings, now put before him a selection of the most peculiar trademarks, a whole library of labels, a cabinet displaying the collection of a sophisticated connoisseur. It then appeared that the outfitter's shop was only a façade behind which there was an antique shop with a collection of highly questionable books and private editions. The servile salesman opened further storerooms, filled to the ceiling with books, drawings, and photographs. These engravings and etchings were beyond our boldest expectations: not even in our dreams had we anticipated such depths of corruption, such varieties of licentiousness.

The salesgirls now walked up and down between the

rows of books, their faces, like gray parchment, marked with the dark greasy pigment spots of brunettes, their shiny dark eyes shooting out sudden zigzag cockroachy looks. But even their dark blushes, the piquant beauty spots, the traces of down on their upper lips betrayed their thick, black blood. Their overintense coloring, like that of an aromatic coffee, seemed to stain the books which they took into their olive hands, their touch seemed to run on the pages and leave in the air a dark trail of freckles, a smudge of tobacco, as does a truffle with its exciting, animal smell.

In the meantime, lasciviousness had become general. The salesman, exhausted by his eager importuning, slowly withdrew into feminine passivity. He now lay on one of the many sofas which stood between the bookshelves, wearing a pair of deeply cut silk pajamas. Some of the girls demonstrated to one another the poses and postures of the drawings on the book jackets, while others settled down to sleep on makeshift beds (The pressure on the client had eased. He was now released from the circle of eager interest and left more or less alone. The salesgirls, busy talking, ceased to pay any attention to him. Turning their backs on him they adopted arrogant poses, shifting their weight from foot to foot, making play with their frivolous footwear, abandoning their slim bodies to the serpentine movements of their limbs and thus laid siege to the excited onlooker whom they pretended to ignore behind a show of assumed indifference. This retreat was calculated to involve the guest more deeply, while appearing to leave him a free hand for his own initiative)

But let us take advantage of that moment of inattention to escape from these unexpected consequences of an innocent call at the tailor's, and slip back into the street.

No one stops us. Through the corridors of books, from between the long shelves filled with magazines and prints, we make our way out of the shop and find ourselves in that part of the Street of Crocodiles where from the higher level one can see almost its whole length down to the distant, as yet unfinished buildings of the railway station. It is, as usual in that district, a gray day, and the whole scene seems at times like a photograph in an illustrated magazine, so gray, so one-dimensional are the houses, the people and the vehicles. Reality is as thin as paper and betrays with all its cracks its imitative character. At times one has the impression that it is only the small section immediately before us that falls into the expected pointillistic picture of a city thoroughfare, while on either side, the improvised masquerade is already disintegrating and, unable to endure, crumbles behind us into plaster and sawdust, into the storeroom of an enormous, empty theater. The tenseness of an artificial pose, the assumed earnestness of a mask, an ironical pathos tremble on this façade.

But far be it from us to wish to expose this sham. Despite our better judgment we are attracted by the tawdry charm of the district. Besides, that pretense of a city has some of the features of self-parody. Rows of small, one-story suburban houses alternate with many-storied buildings which, looking as if made of cardboard, are a mixture of blind office windows, of gray-glassed display windows, of fascia, of advertisements and numbers. Among the houses the crowds stream by. The street is as broad as a city boulevard, but the roadway is made, like village squares, of beaten clay, full of puddles and overgrown with grass. The street traffic of that area is a byword in the city; all its inhabitants speak about it with pride and a knowing look. That gray, impersonal crowd is rather self-conscious of its role, eager to live up to its metropolitan aspirations. All the same, despite the bustle and sense of purpose, one has the impression of a monotonous, aimless wandering, of a sleepy procession of puppets. An atmosphere of strange insignificance pervades the scene. The crowd flows lazily by, and, strange to say, one can see it only indistinctly; the figures pass in gentle disarray, never reaching complete sharpness of outline. Only at times do we catch among the turmoil of many heads a dark vivacious look, a black bowler hat worn at an angle, half a face split by a smile formed by lips which had just finished speaking, a foot thrust forward to take a step and fixed forever in that position.

A peculiarity of that district are the cabs, without coachmen, driving along unattended. It is not as if there were no cabbies, but mingling with the crowd and busy with a thousand affairs of their own, they do not bother about their carriages. In that area of sham and empty gestures no one pays much attention to the precise purpose of a cab ride and the passengers entrust themselves to these erratic conveyances with the thoughtlessness which characterizes everything here. From time to time one can see them at dangerous corners, leaning far out from under the broken roof of a cab as, with the reins in their hands, they perform with some difficulty the tricky maneuver of overtaking.

There are also trams here. In them the ambition of the city councilors has achieved its greatest triumph. The appearance of these trams, though, is pitiful, for they are made of papier-mâché with warped sides dented from the misuse of many years. They often have no fronts, so that

the tailors dummies? has his father's imagination been realized

in passing one can see the passengers, sitting stiffly and behaving with great decorum. These trams are pushed by the town porters. The strangest thing of all is, however, the railway system in the Street of Crocodiles.

Occasionally, at different times of day toward the end of the week, one can see groups of people waiting at a crossroads for a train. One is never sure whether the train will come at all or where it will stop if it does. It often happens, therefore, that people wait in two different places, unable to agree where the stop is. They wait for a long time standing in a black, silent bunch alongside the barely visible lines of the track, their faces in profile: a row of pale cut-out paper figures, fixed in an expression of anxious peering.

At last the train suddenly appears: one can see it coming from the expected side street, low like a snake, a miniature train with a squat, puffing locomotive. It enters the black corridor, and the street darkens from the coal dust scattered by the line of carriages. The heavy breathing of the engine and the wave of a strange sad seriousness, the suppressed hurry and excitement transform the street for a moment into the hall of a railway station in the quickly falling winter dusk.

A black market in railway tickets and bribery in general are the special plagues of our city.

At the last moment, when the train is already in the station, negotiations are conducted in nervous haste with corrupt railway officials. Before these are completed, the train starts, followed slowly by a crowd of disappointed passengers who accompany it a long way down the line before finally dispersing.

The street, reduced for a moment to form an improvised station filled with gloom and the breath of distant travel, widens out again, becomes lighter and again allows the carefree crowd of chattering passers-by to stroll past the shop windows—those dirty gray squares filled with shoddy goods, tall wax dummies, and barbers' dolls.

Showily dressed in long lace-trimmed gowns, prostitutes have begun to circulate. They might even be the wives of hairdressers or restaurant bandleaders. They advance with a brisk rapacious step, each with some small flaw in her evil corrupted face; their eyes have a black, crooked squint, or they have harelips, or the tips of their noses are missing.

The inhabitants of the city are quite proud of the odor of corruption emanating from the Street of Crocodiles. "There is no need for us to go short of anything," they say proudly to themselves, "we even have truly metropolitan vices." They maintain that every woman in that district is a tart. In fact, it is enough to stare at any of them, and at once you meet an insistent clinging look which freezes you with the certainty of fulfillment. Even the schoolgirls wear their hair ribbons in a characteristic way and walk on their slim legs with a peculiar step, an impure expression in their eyes that foreshadows their future corruption.

And yet, and yet—are we to betray the last secret of that district, the carefully concealed secret of the Street of Crocodiles?

Several times during our account we have given warning signals, we have intimated delicately our reservations. An attentive reader will therefore not be unprepared for what is to follow. We spoke of the imitative, illusory character of that area, but these words have too precise and definite a meaning to describe its half-baked and undecided reality.

Our language has no definitions which would weigh, so to speak, the grade of reality, or define its suppleness. Let us say it bluntly: the misfortune of that area is that nothing ever succeeds there, nothing can ever reach a definite conclusion. Gestures hang in the air, movements are prematurely exhausted and cannot overcome a certain point of inertia. We have already noticed the great bravura and prodigality in intentions, projects, and anticipations which are one of the characteristics of the district. It is in fact no more than a fermentation of desires, prematurely aroused and therefore impotent and empty. In an atmosphere of excessive facility, every whim flies high, a passing excitement swells into an empty parasitic growth; a light gray vegetation of fluffy weeds, of colorless poppies sprouts forth, made from a weightless fabric of nightmares and hashish. Over the whole area there floats the lazy licentious smell of sin, and the houses, the shops, the people seem sometimes no more than a shiver on its feverish body, the gooseflesh of its febrile dreams. Nowhere as much as there do we feel threatened by possibilities, shaken by the nearness of fulfillment, pale and faint with the delightful rigidity of realization. And that is as far as it goes.

Having exceeded a certain point of tension, the tide stops and begins to ebb, the atmosphere becomes unclear and troubled, possibilities fade and decline into a void, the crazy gray poppies of excitement scatter into ashes.

We shall always regret that, at a given moment, we had left the slightly dubious tailor's shop. We shall never be able to find it again. We shall wander from shop sign to shop sign and make a thousand mistakes. We shall enter scores of shops, see many which are similar. We shall wander along shelves upon shelves of books, look through magazines and prints, confer intimately and at length with young women of imperfect beauty, with an excessive pigmentation who yet would not be able to understand our requirements.

We shall get involved in misunderstandings until all our fever and excitement have spent themselves in unnecessary effort, in futile pursuit.

Our hopes were a fallacy, the suspicious appearance of the premises and of the staff were a sham, the clothes were real clothes, and the salesman had no ulterior motives. The women of the Street of Crocodiles are depraved to only a modest extent, stifled by thick layers of moral prejudice and ordinary banality. In that city of cheap human material, no instincts can flourish, no dark and unusual passions can be aroused.

The Street of Crocodiles was a concession of our city to modernity and metropolitan corruption. Obviously, we were unable to afford anything better than a paper imitation, a montage of illustrations cut out from last year's moldering newspapers.

Cockroaches

It happened during the period of gray days that followed the splendid colorfulness of my father's heroic era. These were long weeks of depression, heavy weeks without Sundays or holidays, under closed skies in an impoverished landscape. Father was then no more with us. The rooms on the upper floor had been tidied up and let to a lady telephone operator. From the bird estate only one specimen remained, the stuffed condor that now stood on a shelf in the living room. In the cool twilight of drawn curtains, it stood there as it did when it was alive, on one foot, in the pose of a Buddhist sage, its bitter dried-up ascetic face petrified in an expression of extreme indifference and abnegation. Its eyes had fallen out and sawdust scattered from the washed-out tear-stained sockets. Only the pale-blue, horny, Egyptian protuberances on the powerful beak and the bald neck gave that senile head a solemnly hieratic air.

Its coat of feathers was in many places moth-eaten and

it shed soft, gray down, which Adela swept away once a week together with the anonymous dust of the room. Under the bald patches one could see thick canvas sacking from which tufts of hemp were coming out.

I had a hidden resentment against my mother for the ease with which she had recovered from Father's death. She had never loved him, I thought, and as Father had not been rooted in any woman's heart, he could not merge with any reality and was therefore condemned to float eternally on the periphery of life, in half-real regions, on the margins of existence. He could not even earn an honest citizen's death, everything about him had to be odd and dubious. I decided at an appropriate moment to force my mother into a frank conversation. On that day (it was a heavy winter day and from early morning the light had been dusky and diffused) Mother was suffering from a migraine and was lying down on the sofa in the drawing room.

In that rarely visited, festive room exemplary order had reigned since Father's death, maintained by Adela with the help of wax and polish. The chairs all had antimacassars; all the objects had submitted to the iron discipline which Adela exercised over them. Only a sheaf of peacock's feathers standing in a vase on a chest of drawers did not submit to regimentation. These feathers were a dangerous, frivolous element, hiding rebelliousness, like a class of naughty schoolgirls who are quiet and composed in appearance, but full of mischief when no longer watched. The eyes of those feathers never stopped staring; they made holes in the walls, winking, fluttering their eyelashes, smiling to one another, giggling and full of mirth. They filled the room with whispers and chatter; they scattered like butterflies around the many-armed lamps; like a motley crowd they pushed against the matted, elderly mirrors, unused to such bustle and gaiety; they peeped through the keyholes. Even in the presence of my mother, lying on the sofa with a bandage round her head, they could not restrain themselves; they made signs, speaking to each other in a deaf-and-dumb language full of secret meaning. I was irritated by that mocking conspiracy hatched behind my back. With my knees pressed against Mother's sofa, absent-mindedly touching with two fingers the delicate fabric of her housecoat, I said lightly:

"I have been wanting to ask you for a long time: it is he, isn't it?"

And, although I did not point to the condor even with my eyes, Mother guessed at once, became embarrassed and cast down her eyes. I let the silence drag on for a long moment in order to savor her confusion, and then very calmly, controlling my rising anger, I asked her:

"What is the meaning then of all the stories and the lies which you are spreading about Father?"

But her features, which at first contracted in panic, composed themselves again.

"What lies?" she asked, blinking her eyes which were empty, filled with dark azure without any white.

"I heard about them from Adela," I said, "but I know that they come from you; and I want to know the truth."

Her lips trembled lightly, she avoided looking me in the eye, her pupils wandering into the corners of her eyes.

"I was not lying," she said and her lips swelled but at the same time became smaller. I felt she was being coy, like a woman with a strange man. "What I said about the cockroaches is true; you yourself must remember. . . ."

I was disconcerted. I did remember the invasion of cockroaches, that black swarm which had nightly filled the darkness with a spidery running. All cracks in the floors were full of moving whispers, each crevice suddenly produced a cockroach, from every chink would shoot a crazy black zigzag of lightning. Ah, that wild lunacy of panic, traced in a shiny black line on the floor! Ah, those screams of horror which my father emitted, leaping from one chair up to another with a javelin in his hand!

Refusing all food and drink, with fever patches on his cheeks, with a grimace of revulsion permanently fixed around his mouth, my father had grown completely wild. It was clear that no human body could bear for long such a pitch of hatred. A terrible loathing had transformed his face into a petrified tragic mask, in which the pupils, hidden behind the lower lids, lay in wait, tense as bows, in a frenzy of permanent suspicion. With a wild scream he would suddenly jump up from his seat, run blindly to a corner of the room and stab downward with the javelin, then lift it, having impaled an enormous cockroach that desperately wriggled its tangle of legs. Adela would then come to the rescue and take the lance with its trophy from father, now pale and faint with horror, and shake it off into a bucket. But even at the time, I could not tell whether these pictures were implanted in my mind by Adela's tales or whether I had witnessed them myself. My father at the time no longer possessed that power of resistance which protects healthy people from the fascination of loathing. Instead of fighting against the terrible attraction of that fascination, my father, a prey to madness, became completely subjected to it. The fatal consequences were quick to follow. Soon, the first suspicious symptoms appeared, filling us with fear and sadness. Father's behavior changed. His madness, the euphoria of his excitement wore off. In his gestures and expressions signs of a bad conscience began to show. He took to avoiding us. He hid, for days on end, in corners, in wardrobes, under the eiderdowns. I saw him sometimes looking pensively at his own hands, examining the consistency of skin and nails, on which black spots began to appear like the scales of a cockroach.

In daytime he was still able to resist with such strength as remained in him, and fought his obsession, but during the night it took hold of him completely. I once saw him late at night, in the light of a candle set on the floor. He lay on the floor naked, stained with black totem spots, the lines of his ribs heavily outlined, the fantastic structure of his anatomy visible through the skin; he lay on his face, in the grip of the obsession of loathing which dragged him into the abyss of its complex paths. He moved with the many-limbed, complicated movements of a strange ritual in which I recognized with horror an imitation of the ceremonial crawl of a cockroach.

From that day on we gave Father up for lost. His resemblance to a cockroach became daily more pronounced—he was being transformed into one.

We got used to it. We saw him ever more rarely, as he would disappear for weeks on end on his cockroachy paths. We ceased to recognize him; he merged completely with that black, uncanny tribe. Who could say whether he continued to live in some crack in the floor, whether he ran through the rooms at night absorbed in cockroachy affairs, or whether perhaps he was one of those dead insects which Adela found every morning lying on their backs with their legs in the air and which she swept up into a dustpan to burn later with disgust?

"And yet," I said disconcerted, "I am sure that this condor is he."

My mother looked at me from under her eyelashes.

"Don't torture me, darling; I have told you already that Father is away, traveling all over the country: he now has a job as a commercial traveler. You know that he sometimes comes home at night and goes away again before dawn."

The Gale

During that long and empty winter, darkness in our city reaped an enormous, hundredfold harvest. The attics and storage rooms had been left cluttered up for too long, with old pots and pans stacked one on top of another, and batteries of discarded empty bottles.

There, in those charred, many-raftered forests of attics, darkness began to degenerate and ferment wildly. There began the black parliaments of saucepans, those verbose and inconclusive meetings, those gurglings of bottles, those stammerings of flagons. Until one night the regiments of saucepans and bottles rose under the empty roofs and marched in a great bulging mass against the city.

The attics, now freed from their clutter, opened up their expanses; through their echoing black aisles ran cavalcades of beams, formations of wooden trestles, kneeling on their knees of pine, now at last freed to fill the night with a clatter of rafters and the crash of purlins and crossbeams.

Then the black rivers of tubs and watercans overflowed and swept through the night. Their black, shining, noisy concourse besieged the city. In the darkness
that mob of receptacles swarmed and pressed forward
like an army of talkative fishes, a boundless invasion of
garrulous pails and voluble buckets.

Drumming on their sides, the barrels, buckets, and
watercans rose in stacks, the earthenware jars gadded
about, the old bowlers and opera hats climbed one on top
of another, growing toward the sky in pillars only to
collapse at last.

And all the while their wooden tongues rattled clumsily, while they ground out curses from their wooden
mouths, and spread blasphemies of mud over the whole
area of the night, until at last these blasphemies achieved
their object.

Summoned by the creaking of utensils, by their ful-
some chatter, there arrived the powerful caravans of
wind and dominated the night. An enormous, black,
moving amphitheater formed high above the city and
began to descend in powerful spirals. The darkness exploded in a great stormy gale and raged for three days
and three nights. . . .

"You won't go to school today," said my mother in the
morning, "there's a gale blowing."

A delicate veil of resin-scented smoke filled the room.
The stove roared and whistled, as if a whole pack of
hounds or demons were held captive in it. The large face
painted on its protruding belly made colorful grimaces
and its cheeks swelled dramatically.

I ran barefoot to the window. The sky was swept
lengthwise by the gusts of wind. Vast and silvery-white,

it was cut into lines of energy tensed to breaking point, into awesome furrows like strata of tin and lead. Divided into magnetic fields and trembling with discharges, it was full of concealed electricity. The diagrams of the gale were traced on it which, itself unseen and elusive, loaded the landscape with its power.

One could not see the gale. One could recognize its effect on the houses, on the roofs under which its fury penetrated. One after the other, the attics seemed to loom larger and to explode in madness when touched by its finger.

It swept the squares clean, leaving behind it a white emptiness in the streets; it denuded the whole area of the marketplace. Only here and there a lonely man, bent under the force of the wind, could be seen clinging to the corner of a house. The whole Market Square seemed to shine like a bald head under the powerful gusts of wind.

The gale blew cold and dead colors onto the sky—streaks of green, yellow, and violet—the distant vaults and arcades of its spirals. The roofs loomed black and crooked, apprehensive and expectant. Those under which the wind had already penetrated, rose in inspiration, outgrew the neighboring roofs and prophesied doom under the unkempt sky. Then they fell and expired, unable to hold any longer the powerful breath which then moved farther along and filled the whole space with noise and terror. And yet more houses rose with a scream, in a paroxysm of prediction, and howled disaster.

The enormous beech trees around the church stood with their arms upraised, like witnesses of terrifying visions, and screamed and screamed.

Farther along, beyond the roofs of Market Square, I

saw the gable ends and the naked walls of suburban houses. They climbed one over the other and grew, paralyzed with fear. The distant, cold, red glare painted them in autumnal colors.

We did not have our midday meal that day because the fire in the range belched circles of smoke into the kitchen. All the rooms were cold and smelled of wind. About two o'clock in the afternoon a fire broke out in the suburbs and spread rapidly. My mother and Adela began to pack our bedding, fur coats, and valuables.

Night came. The wind intensified in force and violence, grew immeasurably and filled the whole area. It had now stopped visiting the houses and roofs, and had started to build a many-storied, multilevel spiral over the city, a black maze, growing relentlessly upward. From that maze it shot out along galleries of rooms, raced amid claps of thunder through long corridors and then allowed all those imaginary structures to collapse, spreading out and rising into the formless stratosphere.

Our rooms trembled gently, the pictures rattled on the walls, the windowpanes shone with the greasy reflection of the lamp. The curtains swelled with the breath of that stormy night. We suddenly remembered that we had not seen Father since the morning. He must have gone out very early to the shop, where the gale had probably surprised him and cut him off from home.

"He will not have had anything to eat all day," Mother wailed. The senior shop assistant, Theodore, volunteered to venture into the wind-swept night, to take some food to Father. My brother decided to go with him.

Wrapped in large bearskin coats, they filled their pockets with flatirons and brass pestles, metal ballast to prevent them from being blown away by the gale. The door leading into the night was opened cautiously. No sooner had Theodore and my brother taken one step into the darkness, than they were swallowed up by the night on the very threshold of the house. The wind immediately washed away all traces of their departure. From the window one could not see even the light of the lantern which they had taken.

Having swallowed them, the wind quietened down for a while. Adela and Mother again tried to light a fire in the kitchen range. All the matches went out and through the opened access-doc   shes and soot were blown all over the room. We st   behind the front door of the house and listened. In the lament of the gale one could hear all kinds of voices, questions, calls and cries. We imagined that we could hear Father, lost in the gale, calling for help, or else that it was my brother and Theodore chatting unconcernedly outside the door. The sounds were so deceptive that Adela opened the door at one point and in fact saw Theodore and my brother just emerging, with great effort, from the gale in which they had sunk up to their armpits.

They came in panting and closed the door with difficulty behind them. For a moment they had to lean against it, so strong was the storming of the wind at the entrance. At last they got the door bolted and the wind continued its chase elsewhere.

They spoke almost incoherently of the terrible darkness, of the gale. Their fur coats, soaked with wind, now smelled of the open air. They blinked in the light; their eyes, still full of night, spilled darkness at each flutter of the eyelids. They could not reach the shop, they said; they had lost their way and hardly knew how to get back; the city was unrecognizable and all the streets looked as if they had been displaced.

My mother suspected that they were not telling the

truth. In fact we all had the impression that they had perhaps stood under our windows for a few minutes without attempting to go anywhere. Or perhaps the city and the marketplace had ceased to exist, and the gale and the night had surrounded our house with dark stage props and some machinery to imitate the howling, whistling and groaning? Perhaps these enormous and mournful spaces suggested by the wind did not exist, perhaps there were no vast labyrinths, nor spirals, no windowed corridors to form a long, black flute on which the wind played its tunes? We were increasingly inclined to think that the gale was only an invention of the night, a poor representation on a confined stage of the tragic immensity, the cosmic homelessness and loneliness of the wind.

Our front door now opened time after time to admit visitors wrapped tightly in capes and shawls. A breathless neighbor or friend would slowly shed his outer wrappings and throw out confused and unconnected words which fantastically exaggerated the dangers of the night.

We all sat together in the brightly lit kitchen. Behind the kitchen range and the black, broad eaves of the chimney, a few steps led to the attic door. On these steps Theodore now sat, listening to the attic shaking in the wind. He heard how, during the pauses between gusts, the bellows of the rafters folded themselves into pleats and the roof hung limply like an enormous lung from which air had escaped; then again how it inhaled, stretched out the rafters, grew like a Gothic vault and resounded like the box of an enormous double bass.

And then we forgot the gale. Adela started pounding cinnamon in a mortar. Aunt Perasia had come to call. Small, vivacious and very active, with the lace of her black shawl on her head, she began to bustle about the

kitchen, helping Adela, who by then had plucked a cockerel. Aunt Perasia put a handful of paper in the grate and
lit it. Adela grasped the cockerel by its neck, and held it
over the flames to scorch off the remaining feathers. The
bird suddenly spread its wings in the fire, crowed once
and was burned. At that Aunt Perasia began to shout and
curse. Trembling with anger, she shook her fists at Adela
and at Mother. I could not understand what it was all
about, but she persisted in her anger and became one
small bundle of gestures and imprecations. It seemed that
in her paroxysm of fury she might disintegrate into separate gestures, that she would divide into a hundred spiders, would spread out over the floor in a black, shimmering net of crazy running cockroaches. Instead, she began
suddenly to shrink and dwindle, still shaking and spitting
curses. And then she trotted off, hunched and small, into
a corner of the kitchen where we stacked the firewood
and, cursing and coughing, began feverishly to rummage
among the sonorous wood until she found two thin, yellow splinters. She grabbed them with trembling hands,
measured them against her legs, then raised herself on
them as if they were stilts and began to walk about,
clattering on the floor, jumping here and there across the
slanting lines of the floorboards, quicker and quicker,
until she finished up on a pine bench, whence she
climbed on the shelf with the crockery, a tinkling
wooden shelf running the whole length of the kitchen
wall. She ran along it on her stilts and shrank away into
a corner. She became smaller and smaller, black and
folded like a wilted, charred sheet of paper, oxidized into
a petal of ash, disintegrating into dust and nothingness.
     We all stood helpless in the face of this display of
self-destructive fury. With regret we observed the sad

course of the paroxysm and with some relief returned to our occupations when the lamentable process had spent itself.

Adela clanked the mortar again, pounding cinnamon; Mother returned to her interrupted conversation; and Theodore, listening to the prophecies in the attic, made comical faces, lifting his eyebrows and softly chuckling to himself.

The Night of the Great Season

Everyone knows that in a run of normal uneventful years that great eccentric, Time, begets sometimes other years, different, prodigal years which—like a sixth, smallest toe—grow a thirteenth freak month.

We use the word freak deliberately, because the thirteenth month only rarely reaches maturity, and like a child conceived late in its mother's life, it lags behind in growth; it is a hunchback month, a half-wilted shoot, more tentative than real.

What is at fault is the senile intemperance of the summer, its lustful and belated spurt of vitality. It sometimes happens that August has passed, and yet the old thick trunk of summer continues by force of habit to produce and from its moldered wood grows those crab-days, weed-days, sterile and stupid, added as an afterthought; stunted, empty, useless days—white days, permanently astonished and quite unnecessary. They sprout, irregular and uneven, formless and joined like the fingers of a monster's hand, stumps folded into a fist.

There are people who liken these days to an apocrypha, put secretly between the chapters of the great book of the year; to palimpsests, covertly included between its pages; to those white, unprinted sheets on which eyes, replete with reading and the remembered shapes of words, can imagine colors and pictures, which gradually become paler and paler from the blankness of the pages, or can rest on their neutrality before continuing the quest for new adventures in new chapters.

Ah, that old, yellowed romance of the year, that large, crumbling book of the calendar! It lies forgotten somewhere in the archives of Time, and its content continues to increase between the boards, swelling incessantly from the garrulity of months, from the quick self-perpetuation of lies, of drivel, and of dreams which multiply in it. Ah, when writing down these tales, revising the stories about my father on the used margins of its text, don't I, too, surrender to the secret hope that they will merge imperceptibly with the yellowing pages of that most splendid, moldering book, that they will sink into the gentle rustle of its pages and become absorbed there?

The events I am now going to relate happened in that thirteenth, supernumerary, freak month of that year, on those blank pages of the great chronicles of the calendar.

The mornings were strangely refreshing and tart. From the quietened and cooler flow of time, from the completely new smell in the air, from the different consistency of the light, one could recognize that one had entered a new series of days, a new era of the Lord's Year.

Voices trembled under these new skies resonantly and lightly, as in a new and still-empty house which smells of varnish and paint, of things begun and not yet used. With a strange emotion one tried out new echoes, one bit into them with curiosity as, on a cool and sober morning on the eve of a journey, one bites into a fresh, still warm currant loaf.

My father was again sitting at the back of his shop, in a small, low room divided like a beehive into many cells of file boxes from which endless layers of paper, letters and invoices overflowed. From the rustle of sheets, from the ceaseless turning over of pages, arose the squared empty existence of that room; the constant moving of files of innumerable letters with business headings created in the stuffy air an apotheosis, a bird's eye mirage of an industrial city, bristling with smoky chimneys, surrounded by a row of medals, and with a clasp formed from the curves and flourishes of a proud "& Co."

There my father would sit, as if in an aviary, on a high stool; and the lofts of filing cabinets rustled with piles of paper and all the pigeonholes filled with the twitter of figures.

The depth of the large shop became, from day to day, darker and richer, with stocks of cloth, serge, velvet, and cord. On the somber shelves, those granaries and silos, the cool, felted fabrics matured and yielded interest. The powerful capital of autumn multiplied and mellowed. It grew and ripened and spread, ever wider, until the shelves resembled the rows of some great amphitheater. It was augmented daily by new loads of goods brought in crates and bales in the cool of the morning on the broad, bearlike shoulders of groaning, bearded porters who exuded an aura of autumn freshness mixed with vodka. The shop assistants unpacked these new supplies and filled with their rich, drapery colors, as with putty, all the holes and cracks of the tall cupboards. They ran the gamut of all the autumn shades and went up and down through the octaves of color. Beginning at the bottom, they tried shyly and plaintively the contralto semitones, passed on to the washed-out grays of distance, to tapestry blues and, going upward in ever broader chords, reached deep, royal blues, the indigo of distant forests and the plush of rustling parks, in order to enter, through the ochers, reds, tans, and sepias, the whispering shadows of wilting gardens, and to reach finally the dark smell of fungi, the waft of mold in the depth of autumn nights and the dull accompaniment of the darkest basses.

My father walked along these arsenals of autumn goods and calmed and soothed the rising force of these masses of cloth, the power of the Season. He wanted to keep intact for as long as possible those reserves of stored color. He was afraid to break into that iron fund of autumn, to change it into cash. Yet, at the same time, he knew and felt that soon an autumn wind would come, a devastating wind which would blow through the cupboards; that they would give way; that nothing would check the flood, and that the streams of color would engulf the whole city.

The time of the Great Season was approaching. The streets were getting busy. At six in the evening the city became feverish, the houses stood flushed, and people walked about made up in bright colors, illuminated by some interior fire, their eyes shining with a festive fever, beautiful yet evil.

In the side streets, in quiet backwaters fleeing into the night, the city was empty. Only children were out under the balconies of the small squares, playing breathlessly, noisily, and nonsensically. They put small balloons to their lips and filled them with air, in order to transform themselves into red and crowing cockerels, colored autumnal masks, fantastic and absurd. It seemed that thus swollen and crowing, they would begin to float in the air in long colored chains and fly over the city like migrating birds—fantastic flotillas of tissue paper and autumn weather. Or else they pushed one another on small clattering carts, which played tunes with their little rattling wheels, axles and shafts. Filled with their happy cries the carts rolled down the street to the broadly spreading, evening-yellow river where they disintegrated into a jumble of disks, pegs, and sticks.

And while the children's games became increasingly noisier and more complicated, while the city's flushes darkened into purple, the whole world suddenly began to wilt and blacken and exude an uncertain dusk which contaminated everything. Treacherous and poisonous, the plague of dusk spread, passed from one object to another, and everything it touched became black and rotten and scattered into dust. People fled before it in silent panic, but the disease always caught up with them and spread in a dark rash on their foreheads. Their faces disappeared under large, shapeless spots. They continued on their way, now featureless, without eyes, shedding as they walked one mask after another, so that the dusk became filled with the discarded larvae dropped in their flight. Then a black, rotting bark began to cover everything in large putrid scabs of darkness. And while down below everything disintegrated and changed into nothingness in that silent panic of quick dissolution, above there grew and endured the alarum of sunset, vibrating with the tinkling of a million tiny bells set in motion by the rise of a million unseen larks flying together into the enormous silvery infinite. Then suddenly night came—a vast night, growing vaster from the pressure of great gusts of wind. In its multiple labyrinths nests of brightness were hewn: the shops—large colored lanterns—filled with goods and the bustle of customers. Through the bright glass of these lanterns the noisy and strangely ceremonial rites of autumn shopping could be observed.

The great, undulating autumn night, with the shadows rising in it and the winds broadening it, hid in its folds pockets of brightness, the motley wares of street traders —chocolates, biscuits, exotic sweets. Their kiosks and barrows, made from empty boxes, papered with advertisements, full of soap, of gay trash, of gilded nothings, of tinfoil, trumpets, wafers and colored mints, were stations of lightheartedness, outposts of gaiety, scattered on the hangings of the enormous, labyrinthine, wind-shaken night.

The dense crowd sailed in darkness, in loud confusion, with the shuffle of a thousand feet, in the chatter of a thousand mouths—a disorderly, entangled migration proceeding along the arteries of the autumnal city. Thus flowed that river, full of noise, of dark looks, of sly winks, intersected by conversations, chopped up by laughter, an enormous babel of gossip, tumult, and chatter.

It seemed as if a mob of dry poppy-heads, scattering their seeds—rattleheads—was on the march.

My father, his cheeks flushed, his eyes shining, walked up and down his festively lit shop; excited, listening intently.

Through the glass panes of the shop window and of the door, the distant hubbub of the city, the drone of wandering crowds could be heard. Above the stillness of the shop, an oil lamp hung from the high ceiling, expelling the shadows from all the remote nooks and crannies. The empty floor cracked in the silence and added up in the light, crosswise and lengthwise, its shining parquet squares. The large tiles of this chessboard talked to each other in tiny dry crackles, and answered here and there with a louder knock. The pieces of cloth lay quiet and still in their felty fluffiness and exchanged looks along the walls behind my father's back, passing silent signs of agreement from cupboard to cupboard.

Father was listening. In the silence of the night his ear seemed to grow larger and to reach out beyond the window: a fantastic coral, a red polypus watching the chaos of the night.

He listened and heard with growing anxiety the distant tide of the approaching crowds. Fearfully he looked around the empty shop, searching for his assistants. Unfortunately those dark and red-haired administering angels had flown away somewhere. Father was alone, terrified of the crowd which was soon to flood the calm of the shop in a plundering, noisy mob; to divide among themselves and put up to auction the whole rich autumn which he had collected over the years and stored in his large secluded silo.

Where were the shop assistants? Where were those handsome cherubs who had been entrusted with the defense of the dark bastions of cloth? My father thought with painful suspicion that perhaps they were somewhere in the depths of the building with other men's daughters. Standing immobile and anxious, his eyes shining in the lamplit silence of the shop, he heard with his inner ear what was happening inside the house, in the back chambers of that large colored lantern. The house opened before him, room after room, chamber after chamber, like a house of cards, and he saw the shop assistants chasing Adela through all the empty brightly lit rooms, upstairs and downstairs, until she escaped them and reached the kitchen to barricade herself there behind the kitchen dresser.

There Adela stood, panting, amused, smiling to herself, her long lashes fluttering. The shop assistants were giggling, crouched behind the door. The kitchen window was open onto the black night, saturated with dreams and complications. The dark, half-opened panes shone with the reflections of a distant illumination. The gleaming saucepans and jars stood immobile on all sides and glinted with their thick glaze. Adela leaned cautiously from the window her bright, made-up face with the fluttering eyes. She looked for the shop assistants in the dark courtyard, sensing an ambush. And then she saw them, advancing slowly and carefully toward her in single file, along the narrow ledge under the window which ran the length of the wall, now red from the glare of distant lights. My father shouted in anger and desperation, but at that very moment the hubbub of voices drew much nearer and the shopwindow became peopled with faces crooked with laughter, with chattering mouths, with noses flattened on the shining panes. My father grew purple with anger and jumped on the counter. And, while the crowd stormed his fortress and entered his shop in a noisy mass, Father, in one leap, reached the shelves of fabrics and, hanging high above the crowd, began to blow with all his strength a large shofar, sounding the alert. But the ceiling did not resound with the rustle of angels' wings speeding to his rescue: instead, each plaint of the shofar was answered by the loud, sneering choir of the crowd.

"Jacob, start trading! Jacob, start selling!" they called and the chant, repeated over and over again, became rhythmical, transforming itself into the melody of a chorus, sung by them all. My father saw that resistance would be useless, jumped down from his ledge and moved with a shout toward the barricades of cloth. Grown tall with fury, his head swollen into a purple fist, he rushed like a fighting prophet on the ramparts of cloth and began to storm against them. He leaned with his whole strength against the enormous bales, heaving them from their places. He put his shoulders under the great lengths of cloth and made them fall on the counter with a dull thud. The bales overturned, unfolding in the air like enormous flags, the shelves exploded with bursts of draperies, with waterfalls of fabrics as if touched by the wand of Moses.

The reserves from the cupboards poured out and flowed in a broad relentless stream. The colorful contents of the shelves spread and multiplied, covering all the counters and tables.

The walls of the shop disappeared under the powerful formations of that cosmogony of cloth, under its mountain ranges that rose in imposing massifs. Wide valleys opened up between the slopes, and lines of continents loomed up from the pathos of broad plains. The interior of the shop formed itself into the panorama of an autumn landscape, full of lakes and distance. Against that backdrop my father wandered among the folds and valleys of a fantastic Canaan. He strode about, his hands spread out prophetically to touch the clouds, and shaped the land with strokes of inspiration.

And down below, at the bottom of that Sinai which rose from my father's anger, stood the gesticulating crowd, cursing, worshiping Baal and bargaining. They dipped their hands into the soft folds of fabric, they draped themselves in colored cloth, they wrapped improvised cloaks around themselves, and talked incoherently and without cease.

My father would suddenly appear over a group of customers, increased in stature by his anger, to thunder against the idolaters with great and powerful words. Then, driven to despair, he would climb again on the high galleries of the cupboards, and run crazily along the ledges and shelves, on the resounding boards of the bare scaffolding, pursued by visions of the shameless lust which, he felt, was being given full rein behind his back. The shop assistants had just reached the iron balcony, level with the window and, clinging to the railings, they grabbed Adela by the waist and pulled her away from the window. She still fluttered her eyelids and dragged her slim, silk-stockinged legs behind her.

When my father, horrified by the hideousness of sin, merged his angry gestures with the awe-inspiring landscape, the carefree worshipers of Baal below him gave themselves up to unbridled mirth. An epidemic of laughter took hold of that mob. How could one expect seriousness from that race of rattles and nutcrackers! How could one demand understanding for my father's stupendous worries from these windmills, incessantly grinding words to a colored pulp! Deaf to the thunder of Father's prophetic wrath, those traders in silk caftans crouched in small groups around the piles of folded material gaily discussing, amid bursts of laughter, the qualities of the goods. These black-clad merchants with their rapid tongues obscured the noble essence of the landscape, diminished it by the hash of words, almost engulfed it.

In other places in front of the waterfalls of light fabrics stood groups of Jews in colored gaberdines and tall fur hats. These were the gentlemen of the Great Congregation, distinguished and solemn men, stroking their long well-groomed beards and holding sober and diplomatic discourse. But even in those ceremonial conversations, in the looks which they exchanged, glimmers of smiling irony could be detected. Around these groups milled the common crowd, a shapeless mob without face or individuality. It somehow filled the gaps in the landscape, it littered the background with the bells and rattles of its thoughtless chatter. These were the jesters, the dancing crowd of Harlequins and Pulcinellas who, without any serious business intentions themselves, made by their clownish tricks a mockery of the negotiations starting here and there.

Gradually, however, tired of jokes, this merry mob scattered to the farthest points of the landscape and there slowly lost itself among the rocky crags and valleys. Probably one by one those jesters sunk into the cracks and folds of the terrain, like children tired of playing who disappear during a party into the corners and back rooms of the festive house.

Meanwhile, the fathers of the city, members of the Great Synhedrion, walked up and down in dignified and serious groups, and led earnest discussion in undertones. Having spread themselves over the whole extensive mountain country, they wandered in twos and threes on distant and circuitous roads. Their short dark silhouettes peopled the desert plateau over which hung a dark and heavy sky, full of clouds, cut into long parallel furrows, into silvery white streaks, showing in its depth ever more distant strata of air.

The lamplight created an artificial day in that region—a strange day, a day without dawn or dusk.

My father slowly quietened down. His anger composed itself and cooled under the calming influence of the landscape. He was now sitting in a gallery of high shelves and looking at the vast, autumnal country. He saw people fishing in distant lakes. In their tiny shell-like boats fishermen, two to a boat, dipped their nets in the water. On the banks, boys were carrying on their heads baskets full of flapping silvery catches.

And then he noticed that groups of wanderers in the distance were lifting their faces to the sky, pointing to something with upraised hands.

And soon the sky came out in a colored rash, in blotches which grew and spread, and was filled with a strange tribe of birds, circling and revolving in great criss-crossing spirals. Their lofty flight, the movement of their wings, formed majestic scrolls that filled the silent sky. Some of them, enormous storks, floated almost immobile on calmly spread wings; others, resembling colored plumes or barbarous trophies, had to flap their wings heavily and clumsily to maintain height upon the current of warm air; still others, formless conglomerations of wings, of powerful legs and bare necks, were like badly stuffed vultures and condors from which the sawdust was spilling.

There were among them two-headed birds and birds with many wings, there were cripples too, limping through the air in one-winged, awkward flight. The sky now resembled those in old murals, full of monsters and fantastic beasts, which circled around, passing and eluding each other in elliptical maneuvers.

My father rose on his perch and, in a sudden glare of light, stretched out his hands, summoning the birds with an old incantation. He recognized them with deep emotion. They were the distant, forgotten progeny of that generation of birds which at one time Adela had chased away to all four points of the sky. That brood of freaks, that malformed, wasted tribe of birds, was now returning degenerated or overgrown. Nonsensically large, stupidly developed, the birds were empty and lifeless inside. All their vitality went into their plumage, into external adornment. They were like exhibits of extinct species in a museum, the lumber room of a birds' paradise.

Some of them were flying on their backs, had heavy misshapen beaks like padlocks, were blind, or were covered with curiously colored lumps. How moved my father was by this unexpected return, how he marveled at the instinct of these birds, at their attachment to the Master, whom that expelled tribe had preserved in their soul like a legend, in order to return to their ancient motherland after numerous generations, on the last day before the extinction of the tribe.

But these blind birds made of paper could not recognize my father. In vain did he call them with the old formulas, in the forgotten language of the birds—they did not hear him nor see him.

All of a sudden, stones began to whistle through the air. The merrymakers, the stupid, thoughtless people had begun to throw them into the fantastic bird-filled sky.

In vain did Father warn them, in vain did he entreat them with magical gestures—he was not heard, nor heeded. The birds began to fall. Hit by stones, they hung heavily and wilted while still in the air. Even before they crashed to the ground, they were a formless heap of feathers.

In a moment, the plateau was strewn with strange, fantastic carrion. Before my father could reach the place of slaughter, the once-splendid birds were dead, scattered all over the rocks.

Only now, from nearby, did Father notice the wretchedness of that wasted generation, the nonsense of its second-rate anatomy. They had been nothing but enormous bunches of feathers, stuffed carelessly with old carrion. In many of them, one could not recognize where the heads had been, for that misshapen part of their bodies was unmarked by the presence of a soul. Some were covered with a curly matted fur, like bison, and stank horribly. Others reminded one of hunchbacked, bald, dead camels. Others still must have been made of a kind of cardboard, empty inside but splendidly colored on the outside. Some of them proved at close quarters to be nothing more than large peacocks' tails, colorful fans, into which by some obscure process a semblance of life had been breathed.

I saw my father's unhappy return. The artificial day became slowly tinted with the colors of an ordinary morning. In the deserted shop, the highest shelves were bathed in the reflections of the morning sky. Amid the fragments of the extinct landscape, among the ruined background of scenery of the night, Father saw his shop assistants, awakening from sleep. They rose from among the bales of cloth and yawned toward the sun. In the kitchen, on the floor above, Adela, warm from sleep and with unkempt hair, was grinding coffee in a mill which she pressed to her white bosom, imparting her warmth to the broken beans. The cat was washing itself in the sunlight.

The Comet

1

That year the end of the winter stood under the sign of particularly favorable astronomical aspects. The predictions in the calendar flourished in red in the snowy margins of the mornings. The brighter red of Sundays and holy days cast its reflection on half the week and these weekdays burned coldly, with a freak, rapid flame. Human hearts beat more quickly for a moment, misled and blinded by the redness, which, in fact, announced nothing—being merely a premature alert, a colorful lie of the calendar, painted in bright cinnabar on the jacket of the week. From Twelfth Night onward, we sat night after night over the white parade ground of the table gleaming with candlesticks and silver, and played endless games of patience. Every hour, the night beyond the windows became lighter, sugar-coated and shiny, filled with sprouting almonds and sweetmeats. The moon, that most inventive transmogrifier, wholly engrossed in her lunar practices, accomplished her successive phases and grew continually brighter and brighter. Already by day, the moon stood in the wings, prematurely ready for her cue, brassy and lusterless. Meanwhile whole flocks of feather clouds passed like sheep across her profile on their silent white extensive wandering, barely covering her with the shimmering mother-of-pearl scales into which the firmament froze toward the evening.

Later on, the pages of days turned emptily. The wind roared over the roofs, blew through the cold chimneys to the very hearths, built over the city imaginary scaffoldings and grandstands, and then destroyed these resounding air-filled structures with a clatter of planks and beams. Sometimes, a fire would start in a distant suburb. The chimney sweeps explored the city at roof level among the gables under a gaping verdigris sky. Climbing from one foothold to another, on the weather vanes and flagpoles, they dreamed that the wind would open for them for a moment the lids of roofs over the alcoves of young girls and close them again immediately on the great stormy book of the city—providing them with breath-taking reading matter for many days and nights.

Then the wind grew weary and blew itself out. The shop assistants dressed the shopwindow with spring fabrics and soon the air became milder from the soft colors of these woollens. It turned lavender blue, it flowered with pale reseda. The snow shrank, folded itself up into an infant fleece, evaporated dryly into the air, drunk by the cobalt breezes, and was absorbed again by the vast sunless and cloudless sky. Oleanders in pots began to flower here and there inside the houses, windows remained open for longer, and the thoughtless chirping of sparrows filled the room, dreaming in the dull blue day. Over the cleanly swept squares, tomtits and chaffinches clashed for a moment in violent skirmishes with an alarming twittering, and then scattered in all directions, blown away by the breeze, erased, annihilated in the empty azure. For a second, the eyes held the memory of colored speckles—a handful of confetti flung blindly into the air —then they dissolved in the fundus of the eye.

The premature spring season began. The lawyers' apprentices twirled their mustaches, turning up the ends, wore high stiff collars and were paragons of elegance and fashion. On days hollowed out by winds as by a flood, when gales roared high above the city, the young lawyers greeted the ladies of their acquaintance from a distance, doffing their somber-colored bowler hats and leaning their backs against the wind so that their coattails opened wide. They then immediately averted their eyes, with a show of self-denial and delicacy so as not to expose their beloved to unnecessary gossip. The ladies momentarily lost the ground under their feet, exclaimed with alarm amidst their billowing skirts and, regaining their balance, returned the greeting with a smile.

In the afternoon the wind would sometimes calm down. On the balcony Adela began to clean the large brass saucepans that clattered metallically under her touch. The sky stood immobile over the shingle roofs, stock-still, then folded itself into blue streaks. The shop assistants, sent over from the shop on errands, lingered endlessly by Adela on the threshold of the kitchen, propped against the balcony rails, drunk from the daylong wind, confused by the deafening twitter of sparrows. From the distance, the breeze brought the faint chorus of a barrel organ. One could not hear the soft words which the young men sang in undertones, with an innocent expression but which in fact were meant to shock Adela. Stung to the quick, she would react violently, and, most indignant, scold them angrily, while her face, gray and dulled from early-spring dreams, would flush with anger and amusement. The men lowered their eyes with assumed innocence and wicked satisfaction at having succeeded in upsetting her.

Days and afternoons came and went, everyday events streamed in confusion over the city seen from the level of our balcony, over the labyrinth of roofs and houses bathed in the opaque light of those gray weeks. The tinkers rushed around, shouting their wares. Sometimes Abraham's powerful sneeze gave comical emphasis to the distant, scattered tumult of the city. In a faraway square the mad Touya, driven to despair by the nagging of small boys, would dance her wild saraband, lifting high her skirt to the amusement of the crowd. A gust of wind smoothed down and leveled out these sounds, melted them into the monotonous, gray din, spreading uniformly over the sea of shingle roofs in the milky, smoky air of the afternoon. Adela, leaning against the balcony rails, bent over the distant, stormy roar of the city, caught from it all the louder accents and, with a smile, put together the lost syllables of a song, trying to join them, to read some sense into the rising and falling gray monotony of the day.

It was the age of electricity and mechanics and a whole swarm of inventions was showered on the world by the resourcefulness of human genius. In middle-class homes cigar sets appeared equipped with an electric lighter: you pressed a switch and a sheaf of electric sparks lit a wick soaked in gasoline. The inventions gave rise to exaggerated hopes. A musical box in the shape of a Chinese pagoda would, when wound, begin to play a little rondo while turning like a merry-go-round. Bells tinkled at intervals, the doors flapped wide to show the turning barrel playing a snuff-box triolet. In every house electric bells were installed. Domestic life stood under the sign of galvanism. A spool of insulated wire became the symbol of the times. Young dandies demonstrated Galvani's invention in living rooms and were rewarded with radiant looks from the ladies. An electric conductor opened the way to women's hearts. After an experiment had succeeded, the heroes of the day blew kisses all round, amid the applause of the living rooms.

It was not long before the city filled with velocipedes of various sizes and shapes. An outlook based on philosophy became obligatory. Whoever admitted to a belief in progress had to draw the logical conclusion and ride a velocipede. The first to do so were of course the lawyers' apprentices, that vanguard of new ideas, with their waxed mustaches and their bowler hats, the hope and flower of youth. Pushing through the noisy mob, they rode through the traffic on enormous bicycles and tricycles which displayed their wire spokes. Placing their hands on wide handlebars, they maneuvered from the high saddle the enormous hoop of the wheel and cut into the amused mob in a wavy line. Some of them succumbed to apostolic zeal. Lifting themselves on their moving pedals, as if on stirrups, they addressed the crowd from on high, forecasting a new happy era for mankind—salvation through the bicycle. . . . And they rode on amid the applause of the public, bowing in all directions.

And yet there was something grievously embarrassing in those splendid and triumphal rides, something painful and unpleasant which even at the summit of their success threatened to disintegrate into parody. They must have felt it themselves when, hanging like spiders among the delicate machinery, straddled on their pedals like great jumping frogs, they performed ducklike movements above the wide turning wheels. Only a step divided them from ridicule and they took it with despair, leaning over the handlebars and redoubling the speed of their ride, in a tangle of violent head-over-heels gymnastics. Can one wonder? Man was entering under false pretenses the sphere of incredible facilities, acquired too cheaply, below cost price, almost for nothing, and the disproportion between outlay and gain, the obvious fraud on nature, the excessive payment for a trick of genius, had to be offset by self-parody. The cyclists rode on among elemental outbursts of laughter—miserable victors, martyrs to their genius—so great was the comic appeal of these wonders of technology.

When my brother brought an electromagnet for the first time home from school, when with a shiver we all sensed by touch the vibrations of the mysterious life enclosed in an electric circuit, my father smiled a superior smile. A long-range idea was maturing in his mind; there merged and forged a chain of ideas he had had for a long time. Why did Father smile to himself, why did his eyes turn up, misty, in a parody of mock admiration? Who can tell? Did he foresee the coarse trick, the vulgar intrigue, the transparent machinations behind the amazing manifestations of the secret force? Yet that moment marked a turning point: it was then that Father began his laboratory experiments.

Father's laboratory equipment was simple: a few spools of wire, a few bottles of acid, zinc, lead, and carbon— these constituted the workshop of that very strange esoterist. "Matter," he said, modestly lowering his eyes and stifling a cough, "Matter, gentlemen—" He did not finish his sentence, he left his listeners guessing that he was about to expose a big swindle, that all we who sat there were being taken for a ride. With downcast eyes my father quietly sneered at that age-long fetish. *"Panta rei!"* he exclaimed, and indicated with a movement of his hands the eternal circling of substance. For a long time he had wanted to mobilize the forces hidden in it, to make its stiffness melt, to pave its way to universal penetration, to transfusion, to universal circulation in accordance with its true nature.

"Principium individuationis—my foot," he used to say, thus expressing his limitless contempt for that guiding human principle. He threw out these words in passing, while running from wire to wire. He half-closed his eyes and touched delicately various points of the circuit, feeling for the slight differences in potential. He made incisions in the wire, leaned over it, listening, and immediately moved ten steps farther, to repeat the same gestures at another point of the circuit. He seemed to have a dozen hands and twenty senses. His brittle attention wandered to a hundred places at once. No point in space was free from his suspicions. He leaned over to pierce the wire at some place and then, with a sudden jump backward, he pounced at another like a cat on its prey and, missing, became confused. "I am sorry," he would say, addressing himself unexpectedly to the astonished onlooker. "I am sorry, I am concerned with that section of space which you are filling. Couldn't you move a little to one side for a minute?" And he quickly made some lightning measurements, agile and nimble as a canary twitching efficiently under the impulses of its sympathetic system.

The metals dipped in acid solutions, salty and rusting in that painful bath, began to conduct in darkness. Awakened from their stiff lifelessness, they hummed monotonously, sang metallically, shone molecularly in the incessant dusk of those mournful and late days. Invisible charges rose in the poles and swamped them, escaping into the circling darkness. An imperceptible tickling, a blind prickly current traversed the space polarized into concentric lines of energy, into circles and spirals of a magnetic field. Here and there an awakened apparatus would give out signals, another would reply a moment later, out of turn, in hopeless monosyllables, dash–dot– dash in the intervals of a dull lethargy. My father stood among those wandering currents, a smile of suffering on his face, impressed by that stammering articulation, by the misery, shut in once and for all, irrevocably, which was monotonously signaling in crippled half-syllables from the unliberated depths.

As a consequence of these researches, my father achieved amazing results. He proved, for instance, that an electric bell, built on the principle of Neeff's hammer, is an ordinary mystification. It was not man who had broken into the laboratory of nature, but nature that had drawn him into its machinations, achieving through his experiments its own obscure aims. During dinner my father would touch the nail of his thumb with the handle of a spoon dipped in soup, and suddenly Neeff's bell would begin to rattle inside the lamp. The whole apparatus was quite superfluous, quite unnecessary: Neeff's bell was the point of convergence of certain impulses of matter, which used man's ingenuity for its own purposes. It was Nature that willed and worked, man was nothing more than an oscillating arrow, the shuttle of a loom, darting here or there according to Nature's will. He was himself only a component, a part of Neeff's hammer.

Somebody once mentioned "mesmerism" and my father took this up too, immediately. The circle of his theories had closed, he had found the missing link. According to his theory, man was only a transit station, a temporary junction of mesmeric currents, wandering hither and thither within the lap of eternal matter. All the inventions in which he took such pride were traps into which nature had enticed him, were snares of the unknown. Father's experiments began to acquire the character of magic and legerdemain, of a parody of juggling. I won't mention the numerous experiments with pigeons, which, by manipulating a wand, he multiplied into two, four, or ten, only to enclose them, with visible effort, back again into the wand. He would raise his hat and out they flew fluttering, one by one, returning to reality in their full complement and settling on the table in a wavy, mobile, cooing heap. Sometimes Father interrupted himself at an unexpected point of the experiment, stood up undecided, eyes half-closed, and, after a second, ran with tiny steps to the entrance hall where he put his head into the chimney shaft. It was dark there, bleak from soot, cozy as in the very center of nothingness, and warm currents of air streamed up and down. Father closed his eyes and stayed there for a time in that warm, black void. We all felt that the incident had little to do with the matters at hand, that it somehow occurred at the back stage of things; we inwardly shut our eyes to that marginal fact which belonged to quite a different dimension.

My father had in his repertoire some really depressing tricks that filled one with true melancholy. We had in our dining room a set of chairs with tall backs, beautifully carved in the realistic manner into garlands of leaves and flowers; it was enough for Father to flip the carvings and they suddenly acquired an exceptionally witty physiognomy; they began to grimace and wink significantly. This could become extremely embarrassing, almost unbearable, for the winking took on a wholly definite direction, an irresistible inevitability and one or another of those present would suddenly exclaim: "Aunt Wanda, by God, Aunt Wanda!" The ladies began to scream for it really was Aunt Wanda's true image; it was more than that— it was she herself on a visit, sitting at table and engaging in never-ending discourses during which one could never get a word in edgewise. Father's miracles canceled themselves out automatically, for he did not produce a ghost but the real Aunt Wanda in all her ordinariness and commonness, which excluded any thought of a possible miracle.

Before we relate the other events of that memorable winter, we might shortly mention a certain incident which has been always hushed up in our family. What exactly had happened to Uncle Edward? He came at that time to stay with us, unsuspecting, in sparkling good health and full of plans, having left his wife and small daughter in the country. He just came in the highest of spirits, to have a little change and some fun away from his family. And what happened? Father's experiments made a tremendous impression on him. After the first few tricks, he got up, took off his coat, and placed himself entirely at Father's disposal. Without reservations! He said this with a piercing direct look and stressed it with a strong and earnest handshake. My father understood. He made sure that Uncle had no traditional prejudices regarding *"principium individuationis."* It appeared that he had none, none at all. Uncle had a progressive mind and no prejudices. His only passion was to serve Science.

At first Father left him a degree of freedom. He was making preparations for a decisive experiment. Uncle Edward took advantage of his leisure to explore the city. He bought himself a bicycle of imposing dimensions and rode it around Market Square, looking from the height of his saddle into the windows of second-floor apartments. Passing our house, he would elegantly lift his hat to the ladies standing in the window. He had a twirled, upturned mustache and a small pointed beard. Soon, however, Uncle discovered that a bicycle could not introduce him into the deeper secrets of mechanics, that that astonishing machine was unable to provide lasting metaphysical thrills. And then the experiments began, based on the *"principium individuationis."* Uncle Edward had no objections at all to being physically reduced, for the benefit of science, to the bare principle of Neeff's hammer. He agreed without regret to a gradual shedding of all his characteristics in order to lay bare his deepest self, in harmony, as he had felt for a long time, with that very principle.

Having shut himself in his study, Father began the gradual penetration into Uncle Edward's complicated essence by a tiring psychoanalysis that lasted for many days and nights. The table of the study began to fill with the isolated complexes of Edward's ego. At first Uncle, although much reduced, turned up for meals and tried to take part in our conversations. He also went once more for a ride on his bicycle, but soon gave it up as he felt rather incomplete. A kind of shame took hold of him, characteristic for the stage at which he found himself. He began to shun people. At the same time, Father was getting ever nearer to his objective. He had reduced Uncle to the indispensable minimum, by removing from him one by one all the inessentials. He placed him high in a wall recess in the staircase, arranging his elements in accordance with the principle of Leclanche's reaction. The wall in that place was moldy and white mildew showed on it. Without any scruples Father took advantage of the entire stock of Uncle's enthusiasm, he spread his flex along the length of the entrance hall and the left wing of the house. Armed with a pair of steps he drove small nails into the wall of the dark passage, along the whole path of Uncle's present existence. Those smoky, yellow afternoons were almost completely dark. Father used a lighted candle with which he illuminated the mildewy wall at close quarters, inch by inch. I have heard it said that at the last moment Uncle Edward, until then heroically composed, showed a certain impatience. They say that there was even a violent, although belated, explosion that very nearly ruined the almost completed work. But the installation was ready and Uncle Edward, who all his life had been a model husband, father, and businessman, eventually submitted with dignity to his final role.

Uncle functioned excellently. There was no instance of his refusal to obey. Having discarded his complicated personality, in which at one time he had lost himself, he found at last the purity of a uniform and straightforward guiding principle to which he was subjected from now on. At the cost of his complexity, which he could manage only with difficulty, he had now achieved a simple problem-free immortality. Was he happy? One would ask that question in vain. A question like this makes sense only when applied to creatures who are rich in alternative possibilities, so that the actual truth can be contrasted with partly real probabilities and reflect itself in them. But Uncle Edward had no alternatives; the dichotomy "happy/unhappy" did not exist for him because he had been completely integrated. One had to admit to a grudging approval when one saw how punctually, how accurately he was functioning. Even his wife, Aunt Teresa, who followed him to our city, could not stop herself from pressing the button quite often, in order to hear that loud and sonorous sound in which she recognized the former timbre of her husband's voice in moments of irritation. As to their daughter, Edy, one might say that she was fascinated by her father's career. Later, it is true, she took it out on me, avenging my father's action, but that is part of a different story.

2

The days passed, the afternoons grew longer: there was nothing to do in them. The excess of time, still raw, still sterile and without use, lengthened the evenings with empty dusks. Adela, after washing up early and clearing the kitchen, stood idly on the balcony looking vacantly at the pale redness of the evening distance. Her beautiful eyes, so expressive at other times, were blank from dull reveries, protruding, large, and shining. Her complexion, at the end of winter matted and gray from kitchen smells, now, under the influence of the spring-ward gravitation of the moon, which was waxing from quarter to quarter, became younger, acquired milky reflexes, opaline shades, and the glaze of enamel. She now had the whip hand over the shop assistants, who cringed under her dark looks, discarded the role of would-be cynics, frequenters of city taverns and other places of ill-repute, and, enraptured by her new beauty, sought a different method of approach, ready to make concessions toward putting the relationship on a new basis and to recognize positive facts.

Father's experiments did not, in spite of expectations, produce any revolution in the life of the community. The grafting of mesmerism on the body of modern physics did not prove fertile. It was not because there was no grain of truth in Father's discoveries. But truth is not a decisive factor for the success of an idea. Our metaphysical hunger is limited and can be satisfied quickly. Father was just standing on the threshold of new revelations when we, the ranks of his adherents and followers, began to succumb to discouragement and anarchy. The signs of impatience became more and more frequent: there were even open protestations. Our nature rebelled against the relaxation of fundamental laws; we were fed up with miracles and wished to return to the old, familiar, solid prose of the eternal order. And Father understood this. He understood that he had gone too far, and put a rein on the flight of his fancies. The circle of elegant female disciples and male followers with waxed mustaches began to melt away day by day. Father, wishing to withdraw with honor, was intending to give a final concluding lecture, when suddenly a new event turned everybody's attention in a completely unexpected direction.

One day my brother, on his return from school, brought the improbable and yet true news of the imminent end of the world. We asked him to repeat it, thinking that we had misheard. We hadn't. This is what that incredible, that completely baffling piece of news was: unready and unfinished, just as it was, at a random point in time and space, without closing its accounts, without having reached any goal, in mid-sentence as it were, without a period or exclamation mark, without a last judgment or God's Wrath—in an atmosphere of friendly understanding, loyally, by mutual agreement and in accordance with rules observed by both parties—the world was to be hit on the head, simply and irrevocably. No, it was not to be an eschatological, tragic finale as forecast long ago by the prophets, nor the last act of the *Divine Comedy*. No. It was to be a trick cyclist's, a prestidigitator's, end of the world, splendidly hocus-pocus and bogus-experimental—accompanied by the plaudits of all the spirits of Progress. There was almost no one to whom the idea would not appeal. The frightened, the protesters, were immediately hushed up. Why did not they understand that this was a simply incredible chance, the most progressive, freethinking end of the world imaginable, in line with the spirit of the times, an honorable end, a credit to the Supreme Wisdom? People discussed it with enthusiasm, drew pictures *"ad oculos"* on pages torn from pocket notebooks, provided irrefutable proofs, knocking their opponents and the skeptics out of the ring. In illustrated journals whole-page pictures began to appear, drawings of the anticipated catastrophe with effective staging. These usually represented panic-stricken populous cities under a night sky resplendent with lights and astronomical phenomena. One saw already the astonishing action of the distant comet, whose parabolic summit remained in the sky in immobile flight, still pointing toward the earth, and approaching it at a speed of many miles per second. As in a circus farce, hats and bowlers rose into the air, hair stood on end, umbrellas opened by themselves, and bald patches were disclosed under escaping wigs—and above it all there spread a black enormous sky, shimmering with the simultaneous alert of all the stars.

Something festive had entered our lives, an eager enthusiasm. An importance permeated our gestures and swelled our chests with cosmic sighs. The earthly globe seethed at night with a solemn uproar from the unanimous ecstasy of thousands. The nights were black and vast. The nebulae of stars around the earth became more numerous and denser. In the dark interplanetary spaces these stars appeared in different positions, strewing the dust of meteors from abyss to abyss. Lost in the infinite, we had almost forsaken the earthly globe under our feet; we were disoriented, losing our bearings; we hung head-down like antipodes over the upturned zenith and wandered over the starry heaps, moving a wetted finger across maps of the sky, from star to star. Thus we meandered in extended, disorderly, single file, scattering in all directions on the rungs of the infinite ladders of the night —emigrants from the abandoned globe, plundering the immense antheap of stars. The last barriers fell, the cyclists rode into stellar space, rearing on their vehicles, and were perpetuated in an immobile flight in the interplanetary vacuum, which revealed ever new constellations. Thus circling on an endless track, they marked the paths of a sleepless cosmography, while in reality, black as soot, they succumbed to a planetary lethargy, as if they had put their heads into the fireplace, the final goal of all those blind flights.

After short, incoherent days, partly spent in sleeping, the nights opened up like an enormous, populated motherland. Crowds filled the streets, turned out in public squares, head close to head, as if the top of a barrel of caviar had been removed and it was now flowing out in a stream of shiny buckshot, a dark river under a pitch-black night noisy with stars. The stairs broke under the weight of thousands, at all the upper floor windows little figures appeared, matchstick people jumping over the rails in a moon-struck fervor, making living chains, like ants, living structures and columns—one astride another's shoulders—flowing down from windows to the platforms of squares lit by the glare of burning tar barrels.

I must beg forgiveness if in describing these scenes of enormous crowds and general uproar, I tend to exaggerate, modeling myself unwittingly on certain old engravings in the great book of disasters and catastrophes of the human species. But they all create a pre-image and the megalomanic exaggeration, the enormous pathos of all these scenes proved that we had removed the bottom of the eternal barrel of memories, of an ultra-barrel of myth, and had broken into a prehuman night of untamed elements, of incoherent anamnesis, and could not hold back the swelling flood. Ah, these nights filled with stars shimmering like fishscales! Ah, these banks of mouths incessantly swallowing in small gulps, in hungry draught, the swelling undrunk streams of those dark rain-drenched nights! In what fatal nets, in what miserable trammels did those multiplicated generations end?

Oh, skies of those days, skies of luminous signals and meteors, covered by the calculations of astronomers, copied a thousand times, numbered, marked with the watermarks of algebra! With faces blue from the glory of those nights, we wandered through space pulsating from the explosions of distant suns, in a sidereal brightness—human ants, spreading in a broad heap on the sandbanks of the milky way spilled over the whole sky—a human river overshadowed by the cyclists on their spidery machines. Oh, stellar arena of night, scarred by the evolutions, spirals and leaps of those nimble riders; oh, cycloids and epi-cycloids executed in inspiration along the diagonals of the sky, amid lost wire spokes, hoops shed with indifference, to reach the bright goal denuded, with nothing but the pure idea of cycling! From these days dates a new constellation, the thirteenth group of stars, included forever in the zodiac and resplendent since then in the firmament of our nights: THE CYCLIST.

The houses, wide open at night during that time, remained empty in the light of violently flickering lamps. The curtains blew out far into the night and the rows of rooms stood in an all-embracing, incessant draft, which shot through them in violent, relentless alarm. It was Uncle Edward sounding the alert. Yes, at last he had lost patience, cut off his bonds, trod down the categorical imperative, broken away from the rigors of high morals, and sounded the alarm. One tried to silence him with the help of a long stick, one put kitchen rags to stop the violent explosions of sound. But even gagged in this way he never stopped agitating, he rang madly, without respite, without heed that his life was flowing away from him in the continuous rattling, that he was bleeding white in everybody's sight, beyond help, in a fatal frenzy.

Occasionally someone would rush into the empty rooms pierced by that devilish ringing under the glowing lamps, take a few hesitant steps on tiptoe and stop abruptly as if looking for something. The mirrors took him speechlessly into their transparent depths and divided him in silence between themselves. Uncle Edward was ringing to high heaven through all these bright and empty rooms. The lonely deserter from the stars, conscience stricken, as if he had come to commit an evil deed, retreated stealthily from the flat, deafened by the constant ringing. He went to the front door accompanied by the vigilant mirrors which let him through their shiny ranks, while into their depth there tiptoed a swarm of doubles with fingers to their lips.

Again the sky opened above us with its vastness strewn with stellar dust. In that sky, at an early hour of each night appeared that fatal comet, hanging aslant, at the apex of its parabola, aiming unerringly at the earth and swallowing many miles per second. All eyes were directed at him, while he, shining metallically, oblong in shape, slightly brighter in his protuberant middle, performed his daily work with mathematical precision. How difficult it was to believe that that small worm, innocently glowing among the innumerable swarms of stars, was the fiery finger from Belshazzar's feast, writing on the blackboard of the sky the perdition of our globe. But every child knew by heart the fatal formula expressed in the logarithm of a multiple integer, from which our inescapable destruction would result. What was there to save us?

While the mob scattered in the open, losing itself under the starry lights and celestial phenomena, my father remained stealthily at home. He was the only one who knew a secret escape from our trap, the back door of cosmology. He smiled secretly to himself. While Uncle Edward, choked with rags, was desperately sounding the alarm, Father silently put his head into the chimney shaft of the stove. It was black and quiet there. It smelled of warm air, of soot, of silence, of stillness. Father made himself comfortable and sat blissfully, his eyes closed. Into that black carapace of the house, emerging over the roof into the starry night, there entered the frail light of a star and breaking as if in the glass of a telescope lit a spark in the hearth, a tiny seed in the dark retort of the chimney. Father was slowly turning the screw of a microscope and the fatal creation, bright like the moon, brought near to arm's length by the lens, plastic and shining with a limestone relief in the silent blackness of planetary emptiness, moved into the field of vision. It was slightly scrofulous, somewhat pockmarked—that brother of the moon, his lost double, returning after a thousand years of wandering to the motherland of the Earth. My father moved it closer to his protruding eye: it was like a slice of Gruyère cheese riddled with holes, pale yellow, sharply lit, covered with white, leprous spots. His hand on the screw of the microscope, his gaze blinded by the light of the oculars, my father moved his cold eyes on the limestone globe, he saw on its surface the complicated print of the disease gnawing at it from inside, the curved channels of the bookworm, burrowing under the cheesy, unhealthy surface. Father shivered and saw his mistake: no, this was not Gruyère cheese, this was obviously a human brain, an anatomical crosscut preparation of the brain in all its complicated structure. Concentrating his gaze, he could even decipher the tiny letters of captions running in all directions on the complicated map of the hemisphere. The brain seemed to have been chloroformed, deeply asleep, and blissfully smiling in its sleep. Intrigued by its expression, my father saw the essence of the phenomenon through the complex surface print and again smiled to himself. There is no telling what one can discover in one's own familiar chimney, black like tobacco ash. Through the coils of gray substance, through the minute granulations, Father saw the clearly visible contours of an embryo in a characteristic head-over-heels position, with fists next to its face, sleeping upside-down its blissful sleep in the light waters of amnion. Father left it in that position. He rose with relief and shut the trap door of the flue.

Thus far and no further. But what has become of the end of the world, that splendid finale, after the magnificently developed introduction? Downcast eyes and a smile. Was there a slip in calculation, a small mistake in addition, a printer's error when the figures were being printed? Nothing of the sort. The calculations were correct, there was no fault in the column of figures. What had happened then? Please listen. The comet proceeded bravely, rode fast like an ambitious horse in order to reach the finish line on time. The fashion of the season ran with him. For a time, he took the lead of the era, to which he lent his shape and name. Then the two gallant mounts drew even and ran neck-to-neck in a strained gallop, our hearts beating in fellow feeling with them. Later on, fashion overtook by a nose and outstripped the indefatigable bolide. That millimeter decided the fate of the comet. It was doomed, it has been outdistanced forever. Our hearts now ran along with fashion, leaving the splendid comet behind. We looked on indifferently as he became paler, smaller, and finally sank resignedly to a point just above the horizon, leaned over to one side, trying in vain to take the last bend of its parabolic course, distant and blue, rendered harmless for ever. He was unplaced in the race, the force of novelty was exhausted, nobody cared any more for a thing that had been outstripped so badly. Left to itself, it quietly withered away amid universal indifference.

With heads hung low we reverted to our daily tasks,

richer by one more disappointment. The cosmic perspectives were hurriedly rolled down, life returned to its normal course. We rested at that time by day and by night, making good for the lost time of sleep. We lay flat on our backs in already dark houses, heavy with sleep, lifted up by our breathing to the blind paths of starless dreams. Thus floating, we undulated—squeaky bellies, bagpipes and flutes, snoring our way through the pathless tracts of the starless nights. Uncle Edward had been silenced forever. There still remained in the air the echo of his alarmed despair, but he himself was alive no more. Life had flowed out of him in that paroxysm of frenzy, the circuit had opened, and he himself stepped out unhindered onto the higher rungs of immortality.

In the dark apartment my father alone was awake, wandering silently through the rooms filled with the sing-song of sleep. Sometimes he opened the door of the flue and looked grinning into its dark abyss, where a smiling homunculus slept forever its luminous sleep, enclosed in a glass capsule, bathed in fluorescent light, already adjudged, erased, filed away, another record card in the immense archives of the sky.